# A BRIDGE OF DREAMS

# A BRIDGE OF DREAMS

## Asian Tales

Ezra Kyrill Erker

ORCHID PRESS

Ezra Kyrill Erker
A BRIDGE OF DREAMS: Asian Tales

First edition, copyright © Ezra Kyrill Erker 2012

ORCHID PRESS
P.O. Box 1046,
Silom Post Office,
Bangkok 10504, Thailand

*www.orchidbooks.com*

ISBN  978-974-524-148-0

# CONTENTS

# ACKNOWLEDGEMENTS

"Weekend with the Boy" was previously published in *Carve Magazine* and the *Carve Anthology*. "The Lift" and "The Housekeeper" were published in the *Bangkok Post*.

To Elisabeth Rose, Erik Hans Karl Otto, Kyra Else Therese and Paulus Henricus Benedictus for their love and support.

And many thanks are owed to Joshua Raub, Marcel Barang, Belle Crawford and John Larkin for comments that improved individual stories along the way, or for encouragement without which this book wouldn't have reached its present form.

# WEEKEND WITH THE BOY

I get a phone call from the past saying, "It's time your son met his father." There's not a whole lot I can do because she's flown him halfway round the world for the purpose. I remember some letter a couple months back, and it getting misplaced and forgotten and, knowing how busy I am, surely she should have expected as much. From experience I've found most worries disappear when you stop worrying about them.

Then she calls and says, "Well, we're here."

"Who's where?"

"We're staying with my friend Nikki, the one I told you about. Let me know a good time tomorrow and I'll bring him around."

In our short exchange Elaine asks no question, makes no request, and I wonder what once drove me to love a woman who contributes to the conversation nothing but demands. When you impose yourself out of the bluest of blues a more conciliatory approach is in order.

Of course I'd like to meet the boy, but I'm a private man with little enough time for myself, and on the phone I get a little agitated and Elaine gets a little heated saying I told you two months ago, and this and that, as if blaming on me all miscommunications in human history. It's a bit rich coming from her, but then I've always made it a point to be accommodating of the hysterics of women.

So a bony eleven-year-old with a running nose and a bowl haircut arrives on the doorstep still clinging to the hand of Elaine, who after all these years looks almost the same. The idea that I've fathered this boy who can't even look at me is almost amusing, and I wonder if I should have paid all that money to Elaine a few years back without asking for a test to prove he's mine.

"I'm sorry I can't stay with the two of you," she says, "but Nikki already got an appointment at the Homestead Clinic for the two of us, and those people aren't very flexible, and – anyway, you'll have a good time together."

In Elaine's mind she must think abandoning her boy with me for three days is good for us. Or it fits her scheme of how things can work. I've long ago given up trying to follow her logic.

"I'll be back Monday to pick him up." She pauses, and before going out adds to me in a whisper, "Be careful with him. He's a little sensitive."


I met Elaine in Florence, we were travellers, a young American with long brown hair, a thirty-eight-year-old Australian. She was an art history student in Rome. She'd come on a day trip with some classmates to see the paintings and we met in the Uffizi Gallery under a Botticelli. To a friend she was whispering something about symbolism, saying the sea was the Eternal Feminine, a celebration of woman's cool triumph after man's sexual exhaustion – or some nonsense you can only pick up in art history classes. I'm normally reticent with strangers but in this case had to interrupt, pleading that a great painting must be *felt*, understood intuitively rather than analysed with preconceptions. For that is how paintings are created: there is no road of formulas you can methodically steer in order to create an immortal work of art; rather, the work comes out of the artist's soul. Textbook vocabulary merely reduces a living painting back to dead formula.

Elaine was impressed enough by my conviction to give me her phone number.

When two weeks later I headed south and passed through Rome, we met for coffee. She taught me the plural of our drink was *cappuccini*. She showed me the Colosseum. I bought a bronze lion from a souvenir stand which, giggling, we named the Beast. I dropped her off at her student flat, following her up for another coffee. We talked haltingly about music and leaving our countries and anything but art. Her mother was Burmese, her father Italian, she explained; they met in Mandalay and through his work ended up in Honolulu. I was parts German and Scottish, I said less impressively. There was a tension in the room I wasn't strong enough to navigate, so awkwardly, I said goodbye. From her fourth storey window she leaned out and shouted down at me.

"You've forgotten the Beast!"

I ran up the stairs again, two at a time, and at the top she met me, and we kissed, embraced and in that moment felt something undying.

In the morning I decided to spend another day in Rome, before I travelled onwards, to Greece, into my work. Elaine understood I couldn't stay. If we had lost touch it would have remained the sweetest memory of my entire travels, that day wandering the alleys of Rome, sun shining, then making love again in the high grass of a forgotten field.


The boy's name is Joe. A silly name for the son of an artist. I prefer "boy", because at least it approximates the creature. Joe, scrawny and bowl-haired, with oversized clothes and a small Burmese nose, looks nothing at all like a Joe.

I don't know what to say to him. He doesn't seem happy or unhappy to be here, he follows me around as I show him my flat without a word, nose dribbling, then saying, "That's a nice painting," as he singles out the most mediocre piece in the entire place, a gift from a student showing a rowboat leaving a tropical island and heading for deep dark ocean.

I show him a diary of mine, completed over a decade ago with an entry dated from Santorini, 7 April, 1995, in which I wrote, *And, my God, I still love Elaine.*

"You were born out of great love," I explain to the boy in trembling sincerity, but he doesn't seem particularly impressed, head tilting in what could be a shrug. "You were conceived in Rome," I continue lightly. "That makes you a Roman!" I jab playfully at his shoulder, which seems to shock rather than relax him.

His indifference to my efforts is making me nervous, and when he stands there looking at his feet, I begin to resent the judgements he's making against me.

"How's school?"

"Fine."

"What are you learning?"

"Stuff."

"You like your teachers?"

"We have one teacher. She's OK."

"You have some good friends in your class?

"Not really."

"Well, you want to see what I'm working on?"

"OK."

I show him my latest painting, which happens to be *Nude Before the Act.* It's a variation of one of my most recognized pieces and I'm proud of the entire series. But he stands there, looking at it impassively, or uncomfortably. Don't boys like to see naked women?

I can't explain to him that this isn't some personal choice, like I've chosen work over fatherhood. Sons and lovers and my own needs pale in significance with the forces that have given me this human flaw and continue to drag me over the coals with it. I can't explain it and I can't expect him to understand.

So I tell him how I'm able to make judgements on people based on their reception to my art – those unimpressed are also uncultured and brainwashed by the fucking brainless popular culture. I get a little agitated, which is the only way to be when discussing absurdity, and again the boy is unresponsive.

"So what do you think?" I ask him.

"Good."

What do you like about it? I should ask, but I doubt he would have an answer.

Of course I see in the oppressively silent boy an alternate version of my younger self. It took me decades to overcome a stifling timidity. But the very fact I can understand his reticence means he can also understand more of me than others, that he can recognize if I exaggerate my way out of nervousness, or speak inventions in the face of not having at hand the right words.

When I tell the boy about Sydney life I hear my own voice. I'm conscious of its tinniness. My voice twangs – it doesn't reverberate. The words aren't what I want to say. I use words larger than what I normally use. I say sycophant and nonplussed and prodigiously. I also say fuck and whore. I grope more in the darkness than in the light of language. The boy's silence accuses me of insufficiency.

"So now we're back in the kitchen."

Silence.

"Hungry?"

"No."

"What did you eat for breakfast?"

"Toast. Banana."

He says banana in a nasal American twang that makes me cringe.

It was five years after my Rome visit that Elaine tracked me down, finding my latest number through an art dealer. I was happy to get her call from the States until she told me why she was calling.

"I named him Joe."

"Why on earth would you do that?"

"We could really use some money to get by."

"You think I have any?"

Every few years we had a short conversation like this. Sometimes I sent a little money, sometimes I argued I was sending money into a void; I should at least know who the kid was. Then she'd demand plane tickets for the two of them to visit, and we were back where we started.

There's nothing more to see in my flat, and talking quickly winds down again to monosyllables. I take Joe to see a film. At this point I'm not choosy and go to the only cinema in town that still shows proper films. Even for the boy's sake I'm not willing to sit through his idea of a film, which is some Star Wars Trek nonsense. The timing is good, when we arrive a film has just started. It's Australian, independent and was released four years ago but recently won some award so it's in the cinema again. It turns out to be perhaps a bit erotic for an eleven-year-old, but he slides down in his seat as if he's never seen a naked body before – nervousness hums over his skin so thickly I can hear it. In turn it makes me nervous.

It's a pretty good film. The director has since gone Hollywood and made some piece of crap, but this film moves me for part of it by having a young supporting actress with sensual eyes and pretty tits and by stirring up a bit of anger and a bit of sentiment. Then the film ends, we go for a meal, and the film's emotion already begins to fade. The message doesn't cling to memory. By next week I'll have forgotten the film's impact, will only remember a few details I can raise in future conversation.

But not in present conversation. The boy picks at his food.

Why is the world seduced by film? It's no better than paint. A painting lives with you. It hovers above the sofa in the living room and becomes a companion, or it hangs in a museum and, if good enough, leaves an imprint on the visitors. I must have made thirty visits to Den Haag's Mauritshuis. One dozen to stare at Rembrandt's *Anatomy Lesson*. That inverted hand still makes me shudder. Another dozen to watch Vermeer's pearl-earring girl turn her head in perpetual surprise at my love for her.

Maybe the odd young fool goes to see *Titanic* a dozen times – but would anyone look at a single frame more than twice? The potency of film is in its movement. Like a shark, when it stops moving it dies. But a painting moves too, and it lives forever. A thirty-year-old film is hopelessly dated; a painted masterpiece never loses its vitality. The movement is subtle, registering at a subconscious dream level that has more power. A painting is like a monastic ascetic who will say only a few sentences a year but each of them is relevant and can potentially change your life. But a movie is like an American, bellowing out to the world the latest cliché which he thinks makes him look witty but in fact broadcasts his incapacity for original thought.

Film is too easy, obvious. A scene of a girl walking to school can be enchanting simply because it dances. But a painting of a girl walking to school has a life story in each brushstroke, in every choice of colour, in every detail – book bag, pigtail, fleshy pink knee – stroked tenderly into the canvas.

"What did you think of the film?" I ask the boy.

"Good," he answers, his fingers fidgeting. Then his silence shuts him up again. Is that his only thought on anything? Is good the only word of criticism he can utter?

Some aspect of the film, though, triggers a thought. I don't know what part of the film or what thought. The thought is like a pointed shovel scraping at a sediment of sentiment layered in the brain. A clump is dislodged, uneven, small, but large enough to work with.

When we get home I need to transfer this to canvas. No, not canvas, to something porous, to a slab of wood. I grab a flat piece of cedar from the shed and get to work.

Good painting is connected to dream. The more nights I have in which to dream, the better my paintings become. That might explain why I was a late bloomer. It took me three and a half decades of living and dreaming until I completed the first painting I was proud of.

A shovel and sediment is a crass way of putting it. More eloquently, it is a purity, an absolute that dream imperfectly connects us to. Once in a while it weaves underneath and I get my feet wet. Once a year or so it's deep enough to bathe in. And once or twice in a lifetime it is a torrent, a waterfall so powerful it seems easier to drown in its currents than survive.

Much of the time I simply wait for this trickle to reach me, or I trek through the mountains of my mind searching for it. During these periods it might look like I'm doing nothing, to an observer like I'm gazing out of the window, sipping whisky again or leafing through porn magazines, but in fact I'm waiting for the source of insight to flow my way.

Others speak of muses, bringers of inspiration, but this is too anthropomorphic. There is no person proffering apples of dreams, rather a stream of timelessness out of which every great work of art – and perhaps every exceptional work of science – springs.

Even my son is secondary to this force.

As I work I think I hear singing in the other room. When I need a break, I investigate. Sure enough, he is looking out of the window humming something I don't recognize. It isn't a sad song, rather a little childish, but the way he sings it hits some sad note that reverberates in me. The loneliness a human being feels in the face of an onslaught of absence. I go back to the painting but now it's all wrong. It isn't sad enough, which means it isn't true. It takes me most of the night to texture even the beginnings of truth into it.

By profession and by character I'm an artist. There are things I do well and things I do very badly. I'm poor at names. I can't remember what days the rubbish goes out. I haven't remembered a birthday in twenty years – including, unless I'm reminded, my own. I think I'm a good observer of people and nature. I like to think I see the true colours in things, or rather can almost feel their textures on my skin, along the contours of the brain. (No, that's not right – I can explain my thoughts using clichés, since verbalizing what I feel isn't my forte either.) I'm hopeless in my personal relationships. Women come and go, as if my will were irrelevant in the matter. They insinuate themselves into my life, and then they go amidst a great show of tears and anguish. And then there's always another girl. It has always been this way, and even as I age it continues. Sometimes all these faults cause me great pain – a wall of insufficiency towers up and breaks over me and I suffocate in that darkness. And then I work. I work myself out of mind and time. This doesn't mean my work brings me contentment or relief – I work because no other life exists. Painting at its most vivid is a lifeblood-absorbing experience, like a wound, open, raw, festering. Art takes out of me the strength for most daily tasks, which no doubt includes parenting. If the boy comes to hate me for who I am, then he hasn't considered how much I suffer.

The boy, like me, doesn't seem to like the mornings. He comes to my workroom looking irritated and sleepy. I never seem to sleep much any more and have been up for a few hours already.

"Want some bread?"

The boy shrugs. In the kitchen I take two slices out of the package and lay them on a plate. I rummage in the refrigerator for some cheese. I find some margarine and an old bottle of jam with a few flecks of mould that I scoop into the rubbish. I set the lot on the table with a knife. The boy smears a little margarine on one slice, puts the two slices together, rolls them and starts nibbling at the edge. His eyes move around uncomfortably.

I'm a good observer of people, but have no experience with boys. Except, that is, the children of my lovers. At my age a few of the women I attract now have children they try not to mention too often. These little boys and girls of theirs are abstractions to me, like the near mythical East European or East Asian villages their mothers were born in, or like one's allergy to eggs, or another's phobia of heights. One woman has a PhD in tidal pool anemones; another has a five-year-old boy at home with a babysitter for the evening. These abstractions, besides the details I paint, are all I know of children.

He seems uncomfortable that I'm watching him eat, so I go back to finish my painting. There are a few more strokes to make, a few adjustments, and then I can leave it for a while.


We take a long drive in the country.

I have to take the boy somewhere – he's moped around my flat long enough, casting a silent web of nervousness through it – and I also have to pick up a painting I left in a cottage I bought in the country, near Lithgow. It's a case of two birds and a stone. On the way, I talk about my life a bit, to give him a sense of what adults are faced with. My struggles to fend off the bank, having to sell some of my paintings cheaply just to have money to buy Christmas presents (two or three years ago I sent him a watch with Van Gogh's *Bridge at Arles* on its face that cost over fifty dollars – he probably doesn't even remember!), my fights with one of my tenants – all to give him an idea of the financial worries I deal with every day of my life. He seems unimpressed even by the beautiful stretch of forest we're driving through. If I point out a particularly vibrant texture on a section of canopy or a dazzle of green where the sun catches a eucalyptus at the perfect angle, I can see the boy staring off in the right direction but have to wonder how much he sees. He never complains once along the two-hour drive, though. The girls and models I take here invariably grumble about the distance or need for a toilet stop or pang of sudden hunger. But the boy is a quiet one.

When I ask, the boy mentions a few men in Elaine's life over the past few years, and I wonder how they would have interacted with him. Look, kid, you're my biggest obstacle to shagging your mother! They would have tried to play footy with him (or whatever sports Americans play), or teach him fishing in the hope it would impress his mother enough to open her legs for them. And they wouldn't have known how to talk to him. Hey kid … So you're eleven? You into girls yet? They would have struggled to get more than a sentence from the boy at a time.

I ask him what kind of house he and his mother have in Hawaii and he mutters, without eye-contact, something about government housing, which must be some nonsense Elaine is feeding him. As if America has government housing like some Scandinavian welfare state! The poor kid is forced to absorb whatever reality his mother insinuates herself into.

We reach the run-down little cottage I bought as an occasional rural escape and the boy runs through its corridors as if it were a grand old palace.

"This place is huge!" he shouts. "I could get lost!"

Maybe children, being smaller, have a different take on spatial dimensions.

In the room I've designated as my painting den, my most recent nude is drying in the corner. The boy takes one glance and averts his eyes – as if the sight of a human figure can consign his soul to hell. It's the third time he reacts like this, and it makes me suspicious. Is the kid religious? Is his mother feeding him some nonsense new-age cult? Or just the normal old-age nonsense?

Outside it's getting to be late afternoon. In the new light I start noticing an inconsistency with perspective in the painting and feel a duty to change it. People think artists make art but actually it's the other way around: an artistic sensibility is a conduit for experiences that *must* be transcribed into a more permanent form. The artist is helpless in the face of these forces.

The boy is off in the back or in one of the rooms – I can't well check the entire property, so I get down to work. By the time I find the perfect shade of burnt umber, though, natural light has all but faded, and artificial light is too fickle to be trusted. The timing of it irritates me; the conditions necessary for the accomplishment of art are as temporary as the right mood needed to paint. Both have to be synchronous, and I blame the boy a little for skewing them. If he hadn't been thrust on my doorstep I would have finished the painting by now.

It would be unfair to blame the boy to his face and I don't have to. Maybe he saw me at work and has the consideration not to bother me, running off somewhere to play Star Wars Trek or do whatever boys do on their own. I pull up a chair far across from the painting, light my pipe and pour myself a Scotch.

I have an inspiration completely unrelated to the nude. It's a tiny spark of an idea, and suddenly I begin a fresh canvas, squeezing paints onto the palette and then, when that becomes too slow, straight onto the canvas. I grab one tube after another and squeeze out globules of pure red or orange, working them in with the help of a brush. In a flurry of energy I take the palette knife and smear the background until it is a moving, flowing force of lust that surrounds the intangible girl in the middle and describes perfectly what she feels.

"Are we going back soon?" asks a little voice from somewhere, and the answer is so obvious I don't bother to speak.

A while later it comes again: "I'm bored."

"Only boring people get bored!" I snap, as I'm in the midst of creating probably the most vivid backdrop in my entire history of abstract portraits.

It isn't until dawn that I find the boy curled up in the corner of a room on the bare floorboards.

"Why didn't you hop into one of the beds?" I ask him, but he shrugs. Strange kid!


On the way back I'm almost falling asleep at the wheel, but I feel a little proud that I could finish an entire painting despite the distractions.

"What did you do last night?" I say. To minimize diversions the house has no television or much else that could pass for entertainment. I'm always either there alone painting or, more often, have a lover or model along for a weekend escape.

"Played cards."

"Ah, you found the games drawer. Why didn't you read the Trivial Pursuit questions or something?"

"I didn't wanna make a mess."

"You could have cleaned up – or left it a mess. The girls when they come always seem to do some tidying up."

He has no response, but after a minute of silence asks suddenly, "Why's there so much naked people in your paintings?"

I laugh at the absurdity of the question, then I get irritated, then heated. It is his brainless American upbringing, I tell him, that makes him think the human body is something fucking dirty.

He looks as uncomfortable as I've ever seen a person look. His gaze is into the sky, at the tops of the trees.

"What kind of paintings do you like?" I ask, to bring him back to me.

"Landscapes," he says quietly.


I wonder if it's worth trying to explain things. My own childhood was long ago, I've forgotten the fears and dreams of little boys – but then, he's not so little now, he seems to know more than he lets on, likes to observe and take things in. He already grasps something I never understood at his age – that he still has much more to learn. So I can relate to him as an adult, I think. He might find me strange, a bully even, but he'll understand we're both evolved out of the same human process, linked together by blood.

When we return to my Sydney flat, I think of Frankenstein's creature. Born out of a scientific urge, this being was so overcome by the fact he was unwanted that he turned against everything his creator held dear. Could a child be the same? Could he grow to despise me, vowing vengeance, taking not my life – which holds little meaning to me – but what I hold more precious, mainly the beauty in nature, and my capacity for art? Would he learn the means to destroy it all until I suffer as he does?

I see him as my judge, the man most likely to one day become my executioner. The prophecy of Oedipus lives on as a fear in the mind of every father Laius. The son will kill you by becoming a greater man, by inheriting the responsibilities you in your aged infirmity can no longer manage. The son will claim his mother's love and affection, leaving you with only the scraps of duty. The son will shovel the dirt upon your coffin and inherit the earth.

I look at the boy. Just like I have little control over an artwork in progress, this boy has become who he is without any input from me. And yet he is a masterpiece unlike any other, and I can sign my name to him.

"You should go take a shower," I say.

From his bag he pulls out a change of clothes and a watch. He holds it up. "This is my favourite thing," he says, "so I don't wear it, to keep it new."

It's the Van Gogh watch I gave him years ago, when he still had never met me. I lean down and wipe his nose with a tissue.


He sings in his room. I enjoy another Scotch and look up at a small bronze lion on the top shelf of my bookcase. I'd forgotten it was there. He comes into the kitchen looking cleaned up. I relax a little; Elaine when she comes in the morning won't yell at me that I've neglected him.

I ask him what song he keeps humming when he's by himself.

"I don't know. I think I made it up."

"I can't figure out why, but it's very sad."

"Aren't all good songs that way?"

I smile and shake my head. To disprove him I play some of my music. Greek bouzouki, Spanish flamenco, light gypsy ballads, blues rock. "The melodies make you feel like dancing."

He doesn't seem convinced, so I play some Mozart piano concertos. "He almost never wrote a concerto in minor key, which is gloomier."

"He just tried to hide the sadness better," says the boy.

I finish my Scotch. When I really listen, I realize he's right. It all suddenly seems so sad that a tear almost forms. Then it does form and trickles down and another comes and I kneel down and suddenly can't control it. I'm weeping like a child. What's going on? I weep because I suffer, and because the boy suffers, and since I suffer it's impossible to stop the suffering of the boy. I weep because I hated my father until the day he died, when it was too late to tell him I loved him. And I weep for my insufficiencies, and for my past crimes of weakness, and because of this quiet little boy I don't even know. Maybe one day he too will have a son, and will want so badly for him to know who he is that he'll cry.

Then this show of weakness shames me. I find myself holding a boy who doesn't want to be held, his body stiff, arms hanging awkwardly at his sides. But I feel a little unburdened, and smile at the absurdity of our pose. And I laugh. And then the boy laughs too, and we laugh together like two who've flown the asylum.

Later it occurs to me that in recent years I've felt a full spectrum of emotions – I've wept, raged, roared in triumph and cowered in loneliness. But it has been many years since I lost myself to a neck-arching, gaping-mouthed uninhibited laughter like that.

Is the timeless stream of purity wound in a coil around the boy's solitude? When I laugh with him and when I paint passionately, the force I feel in my bones is the same.

When Elaine comes in the morning to take Joe back she asks, "And how did it go?"

"It went just fine."

"I can take him off your hands now."

I say, "Well, there's really no hurry."

✳ ✳ ✳ ✳ ✳

# THE LIFT

I live on the seventeenth storey. I take the lift down to the ground floor every morning, where I grab a motorcycle taxi to weave me through traffic to the real estate office where I work. When I get home in the evening I take the lift back up to my room. At weekends I stay at my boyfriend's place in Bang Na, just outside of the city. On Sunday nights sometimes I come home with bruises.

A young man lives in my building. Ambiguous ethnicity. Thai or Chinese mixed with farang. He dresses neatly in checked shirts but dark brown hair is tangled. Seems introverted, brooding. I've seen him once or twice in the building's restaurant reading an academic-looking book or scribbling in a notebook. Or passed him on the *soi* as I walked down to the main street. I never pay too much attention; he's sort of inconspicuous. Once our eyes crossed and I read nothing in his – not curiosity or kindness or annoyance, no hurry or laziness, nervousness or joy.

But then out of that blankness something happens.

I get home, walk to the lift where the young man is already waiting. The doors open, we walk in. He presses the button for the twelfth storey, glances at me and presses the button for the seventeenth. He gets out at the twelfth and I continue on to my floor.

It wouldn't be much of a story except I've never spoken to him. How does he know my floor? There are a few possible explanations, some innocuous, some creepy.

1. We've taken the lift together before. I left some sort of imprint on him and he remembered which button I pressed.

2. He spends his evenings watching the comings and goings of his neighbours on the building's cable, since one channel is reserved for CCTV. The pictures flicker from one corridor's surveillance camera to another's. He spied on me. Maybe he got a peeping-Tom thrill out of this. He remembered my floor. He watches me.

3. He works for the management in some capacity and knows the residents.

These explanations don't work for me. I can't remember ever seeing him in the lift with me. I'm no expert on voyeurs but he seems too distracted and introspective to fit the profile. I've never seen him actually speak to anyone; it's unlikely he has contacts in the building.


The next time we enter the lift together, two weeks later, he presses 12 and pauses, waiting for me to speak. I don't. The doors close and the lift starts moving. I think, he doesn't remember. He presses 17. We stand in silence, and I feel a little naked in my office skirt and sleeveless blouse. He gets out at 12. I continue on to my room, where I turn on the television and flip to the CCTV channel. When the images reach the twelfth storey I pay attention but don't see him emerge from any of the rooms.


The third time this happens, nearly a month later, I speak. A little nervously, angrily.

"How do you know my floor?"

He seems surprised by the question. "You told me."

"I've never spoken to you. Ever."

His head drops and he looks ashamed. It's the first time his nondescriptness has solidified into an emotion. "I'm sorry."

The doors open at 12. He steps out. The hem of his black trousers is frayed. He looks down at the unravelling thread.

I follow. "You didn't answer my question."

"I did."

"It was bullshit."

He mumbles another apology as he unlocks his door. Room 1217. As he closes the door behind him he whispers something that stuns me.

Barely audibly, he says, "How can you let him do that to you?"


It's true I have a difficult relationship with my boyfriend. I'm not blameless. He's a jealous man from a political family who can find offence where none was intended, treachery in banality. Sometimes I lie to him to spare him pain. When he catches me in a white lie his rage makes him frightening. Afterwards, he apologizes. Sometimes he weeps.

Love keeps me with him. Or fear of being alone, fear of his fear. When he hits me I don't resist; I'm a rag doll in the grip of an unhinged child. I wait until the fury subsides. The shock hurts more than the physical pain. Bruises linger for days, distrust far longer. I reassure myself it's not because I count for so little in his eyes but because I count for so much; if he didn't love me he wouldn't need to do this. I'd rather see evidence of raw emotion than apathy. He pays attention to me. He sees what I'm wearing. If my skirt is too short I'll hear about it. If I look good he'll tell me. He'll say things like "Wear the red blouse with those slacks," and he'll be right; it's a combination that works. And he'll tell me again I look beautiful. And he'll apologize for his rage last time and explain it rationally. And from his perspective, it makes enough sense that I forgive him.

In the corridor outside the young man's door, I can feel him listening on the other side. Listening is the wrong word, since I'm only thinking. But then again, maybe it's the right word.

"You have to leave him," he says from the other side.

"You don't understand. You don't know him."

"I know you."

"No, you don't."

"It makes me feel bad to see you like this."

I look down at myself. I'm clean, neat, hair tied back, any bruises have faded from the chin or – creeping amoeba-like around the collarbone, across the thigh – are draped from sight by my blue dress. I'm not usually confident about how I look but this time I can say I look better than usual, better than most.

"I'm OK."

The door opens a little. I'm a small woman, and today wearing flats. I have to look up to catch his eye, in the brown depth of which is an emotion I recognize, even if I can't believe in it.

"How do you know so much about me?"

He opens the door wider to let me in. I don't want to offend him. He locks the door behind me with the key.

The proximity feels uncomfortable; I step away, towards the balcony. He follows, closing the space between us.

"You've been spying on me?" I say.

He shakes his head. I'm trembling.

"You know so much about me. Or you think you know."

He pauses. "I look … and then hear things."

"You hear things."

"I think they're speaking. No, I remember something, and I think it's a memory of something people tell me."

"But they don't tell you."

He shakes his head. "I don't know if they do or don't."

"You hear them think it."

"I don't know. I looked at you and knew what floor you wanted."

"Why did you lock your door?"

"Because." The question surprises him as I take another step away towards the balcony, into raw sunlight. "I know why you came."

"I came to demand answers."

He shakes his head. "I thought … it's better not to be disturbed."

"From what?"

"It's OK," he says comfortingly. He reduces the distance between us again, and reaches a hand out. Fine hairs at the base of his fingers catch the angled afternoon light.

I laugh nervously, crossing my feet. "Haven't you ever been wrong?"

He shakes his head. Eyes blink. When he opens his arms, I let him curl me into them.

❊ ❊ ❊ ❊ ❊

# AS I WALKED
# A BRIDGE OF DREAMS

It began when I woke into a whiteness, touching at words that wouldn't form. A day different from others before it, because I could remember it as it unfolded. As if time had condensed from vapour to water droplets. I lifted my arm and turned the hand over, gazing at the blue veins beneath the skin. It wasn't an unfamiliar hand, though I'd never seen it this side of memory. Fingers moved back and forth when I wanted them to, to prove they were mine. When I extended my focus beyond the hand, a stranger was there, standing in the white. He took a step forward and his mouth moved.

You're back.

Two words with many meanings. They meant there were people outside myself. They meant I could listen to sounds and understand them, capable of language, and was independent of the force that spoke the words. Things I didn't know before. Most of all, the words meant I was returned somewhere I'd been before – not a creation newly formed from whatever spark forms life.

I was ... here before? I tried to confirm, but the voice faltered.

Can't you feel that?

I don't know.

You should. As Makoshi is how you know me. Or Max.

I don't know you.

It doesn't matter. His hand rested on my shoulder. You had a shock. But our bond and our task are more important than the length of memory.

After Max came Risa. She is taller than me, with black hair curling around her cheeks and skin taut over bones that look breakable compared to the solid features of Max. Holding a clipboard cluttered with uneven pages. She introduced herself, like a stranger, but like Max placed herself in a context she assumed I would understand.

'Among other things, I'm the link between us and the refugees.'

'Refugees?'

'The ones we're sheltering. They speak an old language, full of tone and syllable. I try my best to understand.'

That she could know different languages impressed me, who barely knew one. I complimented her: she seemed very busy, but could handle many things that were different.

'Not like you,' she said with a laugh. 'You did nothing but radio sets. Building, tuning, encrypting. Clever, but very boring. Maybe this time you'll change.'

Then she looked at me closely, eyes set close to each other, before smiling. 'No,' she said. 'No chance.'

She asked if the sight of anything had brought forth a recollection yet. I shook my head. I told her I wished I'd kept a journal before, to read now into who I was and am.

'No one writes more than absolutely necessary, except when emergencies approach. If they find us it is better they don't know how much we know. We're stronger by being and resisting.'

After thinking about it, Risa added that now might be emergency enough for me to write some notes to help ease back into memory.

'The first days are awkward. Give yourself time to fit the pieces, to gather the fragments of broken glass into a window to the past. It has happened to all of us. Even when it seems clear again the shutters will close and you'll regress. Your impressions can be a bridge back to yourself. You can start by writing that.'

The house we live in is remote and large. Black stained beams cross the walls, visibly holding it up. The wood *feels* old, like the arms of ancestors sheltering us. It's difficult to judge how many generations have passed through these frames. The main room has a high ceiling, underside of a straw roof, and sliding doors of paper separate it from the perimeter corridor and the kitchen, where the floor is dirt. In the middle of the room is a stove for burning wood, and it is always lit because here it's always cold. Wind steps through the house, tapping between shoulder blades, settling into bones. The room has rectangular straw mats underfoot. I counted forty-two of them.

The room they say is mine has only six mats, big enough for me and some clothes that fit me and three sets of shelves with books and equipment I don't understand. According to Max and Risa, the equipment is my specialty. But looking over the room before sleep, I don't feel these things reflect who I am.

There are only two mirrors in the house, and they hang on opposite walls in the kitchen. You can't look at yourself without others seeing you, and when you do your face is cast infinite in the mirror behind you – frame by frame representation of all the expressions you can wear. My eyes look sunken, hollow. If I smile it seems forced, lips rubbed the wrong way. My entire face sits on me like a stranger. And I need a haircut.

I've lived in the house, they say, for some time. It's not unfamiliar, but like the shape of a home you know, recognizing arches or the slope of the roof, from a certain place, from a certain period in history. Or one you've seen in a dream.

When I go outside to see where we are the trees cut the emptiness deeply and evenly. Pines and cypresses cordon the house with skeletons of maple, cedar and birch – Risa told me their names and I remembered; somewhere I already knew the words. Stems hang from branches like white bones where the snow touches, or like decomposing hands, limp and broken, where it doesn't. The ground has patches of snow and isn't level, sloping into a mountain peak somewhere. It's a cold into which sockets and joints ache. My breath wisps away like the past. When I don't move and listen, the silence is deeper than just absence.

The house feels isolated, lonely, but almost fifty people live here. Or only five live here, Max explained this morning when he came to see if I was remembering. He spoke while withholding words, trying not to say too much. He has a large presence despite not being a large man, he comes into a room and makes it smaller. Protruding ears, grey eyes are inescapable as he leans forward.

'The others are refugees from the other side of the mountain. They move from place to place in the darkness, and wherever they are they make it into what home they can. They stay here, like you, because they can't go back. Because of their refusal to part with the truth, they've lost everything else.'

He paused for a moment, looking at me. 'As long as they still remember who they are, Shin, they'll never forgive. Fugitives, walking the peripheries, are the only ones we can trust. Others believe only what causes the least discomfort.'

Since my wakening I've wanted to talk to the refugees. I wondered if I was one too, but they speak a different language. And they don't seem to know who I am like the others do. They spend nights huddled around the fire in the main room or in the kitchen, and days gathering firewood or cooking, washing clothes in buckets outside, sitting thinking against tree trunks. They don't talk very much, and only in muted tones, softly sibilant voices. Even the three children, who have large dark eyes and hold pieces of wood or metal in their fingertips. Or hold a happier time in their minds.

'You said we were a unit of five,' I asked, just to be sure. 'You, Risa, Em, Tom. Who is the fifth?'

Max looked at me not understanding, a narrowing of eyes, tightening of lips on teeth.

'Well, you, of course.'

It made me more unhappy not to be able to fill my part in the daily patterns.

'It will take time,' he said, reading my face. 'We can't force your role on you or teach you because only *you* know. To keep ourselves secret we're small in number, specialized, effective in a whole. We must work to choose and solidify our own beliefs and memories or the wrong ones will choose us, and if that happens our collective past will vanish, and we'll be left with nothing. Without history we walk naked on earth. Remember that, Shin.'

And Max left as he came, moving in and out of my rehabilitation.


Risa took me by the hand in the early days and introduced Tomoaki and Emiko.

'You called them Tom and Em,' she said.

I liked the name Em, the way my lips converge and the sound continues. It seems to defy language. The two have other tasks and are messengers, but look impervious to the cold or the wearing-down of long journeys. Em is short and pale, and running messages has thickened her. Her hair is dark as ink, making her look resolute. Tom must be the older but their ages are impossible to guess. There are enough similarities in features – high, strong brow, tangled short hair, eyes descending into the depths of understanding – to make them brother and sister. I'm afraid to ask. Like everyone here they're focused, preoccupied, without time to explain things to someone who wouldn't understand. And I don't see them every day. They go to the town sometimes and I don't know how far away it is but they never return sooner than a day and a half later. Sometimes it's as many as five days, when I feel the tension of worry rise in Risa and Max. The refugees feel it too, though they understand what happens here as little as I do. Return is greeted with an unvoiced sigh of relief, and work continues.

The five of us eat together when schedules converge. We sit in the kitchen, away from the families, in our presence aware of each other. Today when I spoke, Em's face opened too quickly. Her glance met mine, searching for something. Maybe a connection from the life before hangs between us, which shows in her large eyes or in the distribution of her strength on her body.

'How are you feeling?' Em's brow lifted again until her eyes were round.

I smiled but had no answer, since a feeling is something set against past feelings. I lacked the memories to compare what I felt.

'I'm still not remembering.'

'We have to work harder.' Tom's square jaw moved, not for food but for thinking. 'Every time, they understand better how to erase our history. Or they take us more seriously. The forgetting is more complete. Return takes longer.'

'It's because we're working our way closer. The link we make with the truth is less distorted, so they can reach us and their reaction is more complete. Next time memory slips away,' Risa added soberly, 'we might not be able to find our way back.'

'You *must* overcome it!' Max stood up and leaned towards me. 'Our future depends on your past!'

Risa's words, even when heavy, apply to present discussions, while Max's replies seem to come in any context, to any query.

'Did it ever happen to you?' I asked the table, softly seeking allies. I still didn't understand the *it* I had to overcome, this wasting away of a personal history.

'To every one of us,' said Tom. 'Our struggle is older than memory. But since this five-member cell took shape, Max was lost two times, Risa once, Em twice, you twice now. Maybe more. Usually we began a return to ourselves within a week or two. Judging from your slow recovery, though, next time it won't be so fast. If there even is a recovery.'

'If there is a next time,' said Em hopefully.


One of the refugees spoke to me as she cut my hair today. The language of an ancient civilization. Even if I understood, I doubt she would have the vocabulary to express what's happening to them. Probably they're not formally educated – but then, that's a dangerous assumption to make about anyone. If she used my language, would she even say who she was in my words? Maybe there are concepts no shared, knotted language can unravel. Her heavy face in the kitchen mirrors flared with purpose as she eyed my neglected hair. As she spoke her ancient words I realized there was no distinction between the refugees or my four friends or even the forces we're resisting. Rather than detracting from the resistance, it adds to its weight.

With only a blunt pair of scissors the haircut finished well, I think. Choppy, uneven, but that resembles how I feel. Risa said it suits me. Em offered an inscrutable face. A few of the refugees smiled. No other comments.

The others losing patience, Tom has been assigned to aid my recovery. He seems to be the expert on mental techniques, and I'm hoping I can draw from his confidence. Today he started me off with breathing.

'Close your eyes. Four heartbeats breathing in, eight out. Slow the course of your blood, let it gather the past and bring it back to you. Control each muscle, organ, tense and relax them one by one, respect each aspect of your body, then try not to be too conscious of it. It will limit you … Learn to clear your mind completely, but only so it's receptive to the task at hand. When that happens you might visualize a spinning, geometric shape in the darkness of your mind. That will be the crystallization of a purity of purpose.'

Four ninety-minute sessions today. I didn't understand the hours this took, or the sense in it.

'It takes time,' Tom said.

But I was beginning to doubt him, and he was frustrated with me, briefly shaping his hands into a circle, then linking fingers, exhaling with his tongue fixed to the roof of his mouth. Maybe there was no going back.

As an afterthought, he added something about dreams.

'Remember them, Shin. Right now they know more about you than you do. And when our enemies have taken every memory again, every belief, you'll still have your dreams. They're the safest place we know to hide the truth. Collectively they are a fortress.'

A fortress of dream. In my room I play with the pieces on the shelf. Sometimes it seems I know how they fit together, the heavy elbow metal and the blue glass, the yellow wire connecting the greased wheel to a board of circuits. But as soon as I begin to understand, I realize I don't. I open a manual on transistor sets. In the margins are notes in the same hand as these, so they must be mine, but many of the words I don't recognize. It seems the manual is being rewritten.

'They've even kept us blind to science!' Max told me yesterday, moving arms to add substance to the words. He thinks it's only the simplest technologies they can't reconfigure or sabotage.

I take an old machine off the shelf. Opened, I trace the wires and a burnt-out after-image of soldering them into configurations that mean something. It's not a memory of an event, I think, but of a dream I had.

Turn the page of the manual and more handwriting, but either in code or in another script, another language, dotted with abbreviations in letters I recognize. A lot of M. Max, perhaps, or even Em? But, then, why would names appear in technical jottings or formulas? I discount it until I find T, S, E and L – Risa? – and others. Are we the units of a formula of action that won't work without all units in place? It's such a strange idea I begin to believe it – why else would it occur to me? And even the names themselves could be acronyms for a greater function. It would explain why the work of the group hinges on my recovery.

'In the absence of memory,' Tom told me earlier, 'you can wake into and reconstruct who you are. We won't push an existence on you because it will have less value to you than the one *you* piece together. Inherited, second-hand foundations crumble in the face of what we're up against.'

I believe him but think even telling me such things is a kind of pressure, a moulding. Though everyone agrees we have little time left.

The manuals still have no meaning to me. The lists of code hold no purpose.

I sat for hours today with eyes closed. Counting breaths as my ankles ate into my thighs. Tom added some rhythmic percussion to my ears at low volume, then repetitive human voices in monotone, dipping or changing pitch occasionally, sounds I was encouraged to join.

'Don't think of remembering, don't think at all.'

This was only half-successful, and at the end of it the session had produced nothing, though I felt a little better for the attempt.

Tom told me a story. When his past finally returned after it had been taken a few years ago, he remembered all the way *to the point of forgetting*.

'I had a dream once,' he explained. 'I had slit my wrists lengthwise, deep, watching the blood pour out of me. It was a mistake, the blood and the energy I needed to stop what was happening were leaving me at the same rate. I could only look on, an impotent observer to my own dying. Until even the power to observe slowly faded … That was how it felt when memory left me. There was no pain or sudden shock, just a seeping away accompanied by vacuous horror, every event that had made me who I am slipping from me until I became a hollow shell.'

I sat pondering the implications, and thoughts that had been bothering me for a while.

'When you lose your memory and recover it, how do you know you have the real past back?'

'Of course,' Tom admitted, 'much of memory is interpretation. When it fills in the gaps, though, between what's indisputable and coincides with what the others remember, then it must be fairly reliable.'

He paused, wondering how far to continue. 'Once, when Max returned, he was sure he had been the leader of our cell. And we agreed, because it seemed to work easier that way.'

'Then who'd been the leader before?'

'Me.'

'But Max said the easiest choices to make are often the wrong ones.'

'It's impossible to resist everything. You need a balance between what you know and what you feel to be truth.'

'How can feelings be trusted? Because they're outcasts, Max trusts the refugees. But what if one of them is a plant, and only pretends to be with the others, and is reporting on our activities?'

Tom looked at me strangely. 'They don't think we have the numbers or the resources to become a threat. With control over memory, why would they bother with conventional spying? Anyway, the resistance is a state of mind, an intention not easily faked. Risa would be able to know.'

'How?'

'She can almost smell what a person is thinking. Anyone with the wrong intention would give himself away.'


There are whispers carried through the house on the icy draughts, sometimes real, sometimes imaginary. Two male voices were coming from Max's room, and as I passed I moved closer.

'Weeks now …'

'Danger to everyone.'

'… we need …'

'Permanently compromised … at most a week.'

'Em wouldn't …'

'… talk to Risa … our last chance.'

'When Em gets back.'

'What's taking so long?'

I returned to my room and studied the notes in my manuals. I accepted that the equipment and books are mine, that this was once my purpose. Then I went to exchange one meaningless language for another: I entered the main room to warm by the fire and listen to the refugees. I smiled at the children as they played a game with woodchips on a chequered board. They looked up but didn't smile. The girl only spoke a few words to the others. They had no reason to know me, if I didn't know myself.

Em, gone almost four days, returned today, and everything changed. Something had happened. There was worry in faces, running and gathering of equipment, all done quietly. The refugees noticed the change but didn't know what was wrong. I hurried between people, hoping to be helpful, and faces were made heavy by the fact that I couldn't be.

'It's time,' was all Risa said to me with an uncharacteristic expression. 'We can't wait for your memory.'

When night fell Max addressed the families huddled in the main room. He paused to look at faces, but for them disappointment was already a habit.

'I am sorry,' he said. 'It's too dangerous now.'

The refugees understood. They packed clothes, food, some bedding into rolls to hang on their backs. In whispers they mapped out a plan, a route, a hope. An hour later they were gone, trudging quietly into the trees, going downhill without light. One of the three children held the hand of the woman who had cut my hair. Her daughter. Eyes bore an innocence that held her safe from fear but not from loss. The mother's haircut had felt so intimate that the uncertain sway of the child recreated her now into a shape as of my own daughter, and an absence struck me in the new quiet of the main room. I joined Risa and Em, like them poised on the edge of emotion.

'Where will they go?'

'Anywhere will soon be safer than here.'

Em is the one I see and talk to least, but with her large eyes narrowed she still peers at me closely when we meet. When she smiles at me it doesn't relax her features. I still can't guess her age; her voice and face are young but her experience, her responsibilities, seem solid. The ambiguities in her make her beautiful, but then at other times I'm not sure.

'I'm also the sort of doctor among us,' she confessed to me. 'We were hoping you'd recover before this. It's too important that you do.'

She held a syringe, needle bared, thumbing the piston. The gesture seemed too self-conscious, one she wasn't used to performing. She took my arm and looked at me and wiped a vein clean. Her sigh halted in the middle of its exhale, then continued, like a piece of music written that way. Because I trusted her I expected the injection to be painless, but it wasn't.

'Now,' said Risa, 'go back to your room and try to work. Em gave you a type of soporific. You might sleep. Or, if lucky, you'll be in a waking dream, a lubricated reversal of time. Your brain will slow down but your mind and memories will slide, mix. In half an hour or so you might have a vague idea of who you are, of what you have to do, but that knowledge will only stay with you as long as the dream, and you're unlikely to remember it after. And in this state your defences are weak. If you feel someone else in your mind scream and we'll black you out.'

She didn't elaborate. Remembering the conversation I'd overheard yesterday, some hope in the depth of me sank. Tom and Max came into the room and lifted one of the straw mats off the floor, then opened a door indistinguishable from dirt. Below us was a two-foot wide tunnel, its darkness impenetrable. A darkness so complete it reaffirmed my absence from the mechanics of what was happening.

'It goes through part of the mountain,' explained Max. 'Our artery, our secret link with the other side. Carved over generations of memory. We leave tonight and follow it, and tomorrow we'll be there. Before we leave, though, we need you to finish something you began a long time ago.'

'What?'

'A decoding machine. Without it our plan is a foray into darkness.'

I went to my room to write as I wait. As Risa promised, I'm getting sleepy. But in a way as I write this I can begin to remember some things, see hazily right through to the beginning of my life. It's both reassuring and frightening. A glimpse of the north-eastern town, years from here, where I was born, and the red electric train that ran on tracks around my room. The gene-encoding program I designed to win a Silver Prize, awarded by a state that saw promise in me. Before I began smelling the collaboration against truth. My own collaboration with nature, travel, suspicion, the breach with whatever felt right, until at the edge of a gorge in a wilderness of the mind I caught a glimpse of clarity. And that was where Risa, the recruiter, found me.

Looking at a circuit board now, I remember something Max told me about memory, a long time ago.

'Do you know how experiences are stored in the brain?' he said. 'They aren't stored anywhere in particular. *They are wired into the circuitry itself.* Across the entire cortex neuronal pathways get redirected, streamlined, synapses are discarded, and through this process what you learn becomes imprinted. Think of it as a model for what we are doing to future history. Not a getting from A to B, a final goal, but a process – along whose twists and experiences who you are becomes defined.

Combine the process with others in the group, combine the group with other groups – collectively the changes we bring about are fundamental and lasting.'

I pick up the decoding machine, turn it in my hands. I match it to a piece from the shelf, and feel a pain as sharp and blurred as the candlelight. I know what I have to do. I know who I am. And I know that I'm an anarchist.

Today I played in the snow with Em. We are on the other side of the mountain, near the top. Air is thin, we can see the peak, can see into the white distance. Today was different. Our situation is critical, but I threw glittering spheres of snow at Em and she laughed. Snow was cold against the face, blinding white and smelled of the sun. Touching it was painful, bare fingers spilled in snow, melting. Snow became tears. My memory was on the cusp of being and not; I was waking up and it made me sad. I kissed her because I knew in a while I wouldn't know her again. Not like I used to. And she kissed me. An exchange that felt familiar, so that our arms moved of themselves. We surrounded each other, a clumsy answer to all the questions still eluding my scope for expression. Without speaking we stood in embrace for a liquid time, until the voices of Max and Risa coming made us solid. A row of mountains behind them, shaping an expanding system of light and shadow, as they crossed the sun.

I don't know what happened during the night. Maybe all we did was crawl through the tunnel. My legs hurt. My body hurts. Max showed me a mapping machine I once made. Tom took it from him to look at dials that remained silent.

'Let's hope you haven't lost it,' he said.

I think he meant my mind. But I have. The drug has worn off and I can't recall everything I felt with such conviction yesterday, everything I knew. Which means that as experience it has failed. My entire life's range of knowledge and experience has again been reduced to a handful of days, and I'm a baby born of an illicit union between reality and dream.

I wanted to talk to Em again, but she was working on my machine and on lists on rolls of paper, and she looked at me and in our eyes was sadness. We are far from each other. Because of the work, the cause, or the fact I'm not me again? She doesn't think I remember our kiss. Right now, though, it's a memory stronger than that of who I am, and I can't imagine any cause that could surpass it.

'Tomorrow night,' Max spoke to me, eyes blade-sharp and moving, 'could be the last night of our lives. Of us as we know us. Strange that no one knows exactly how long we've worked for this. But it has been a long time. Even now we're not ready but have worked our way out of the luxury of time. Every moment of history has been a precursor to this one. All that's worth waiting for has its own reason and its own course, and the point that can change the future has finally reached us! Such is the urgency of the *truth*. In pieces they've taken everything from us except the conviction that we're right. Let us hope for a great day – a new beginning for hope.'

I asked if we were going into the city.

'You're starting to remember, aren't you?' he said quickly, studying my face.

I nodded.

'What's your family name, Shin?'

But I couldn't tell him. He had to remind me. I had only questions, and was getting sleepy. I moved around the underground shelter, wishing I could do something.

'What are we fighting?' I asked Risa in exasperation.

She looked up from a blueprint, face shading in annoyance. I turned away, but she stopped me.

'It's OK. Sometimes even I forget. That's the idea.'

'The idea?'

'That's what we're fighting. For the *right to know who we are*, to remember what we choose. When we get close they protect themselves by making us forget what we're close to.'

'What are we close to?'

She curled the edges of the blueprint almost suspiciously. 'To stopping their assault on our pasts.'

'An assault they make because we're close to stopping it.'

'Yes.'


I'm useless to them so just now Em injected me again, explaining it was unlikely to work as well a second time. When she pulled the needle out she looked up with a full, sad face.

'What happens if it doesn't work, and we must leave you here, and you have to wait alone until it's all over?'

What was the worth of an answer given in words rather than the substance of my entire self? I tried to kiss her, but it didn't make her happy. She touched my hand after pulling away.

'I don't know,' she whispered, 'how much of you is based on memory, and how much on false dreams.'

'This is who I am,' I insisted.

But she looked doubtful.

The injection didn't work. I slept instead, the red train circling the rooms of my mind. My four friends have gone, into the valley, and I wait alone for their return. In my short memory I've never felt so much loss. I couldn't wish them luck as they walked down the mountain, say goodbye. I was the hollow one without self. Their burden, but now without anyone.

I stepped outside this hole I sleep in. It's night. With Em I'd begun to believe I could translate the world into a structure of resumed activity, but had only forged deeper into a private labyrinth. Tonight an architecture of moonlight sluiced through the trees but roofed in some screams from the valley. Did I really hear the screams, or were they sounds formed from empty time? My own footsteps sounded too solid, rich with the crunch or squeak of snow or crack of undergrowth. I looked around and gazed out, heart throbbing noisily and expecting something to happen. But the darkness held.

It is a few days, no change. No return of my friends, no return of memory. Sleep is broken, full of anxiety, empty of dreams. I read and reread these notes, but even what I've written feels less me, more the words of a stranger. Sentences are a disengaged string of dead letters and words. I start to doubt everything and have nothing to add. Perhaps I'm the reason my friends have vanished, and I have betrayed them: I was returned feigning blankness but instilled instead with a cancer that made me susceptible, given the right conditions, to betrayal. I don't know how I can think that but the thought itself is disturbing – why would it occur to me unless some aspect of my mind that knows me better than I do thought it were true? The guilt lies in the absence of knowing. I wake up with hands still clutching the blankets that the instinct inherent in dreams has kept me wrapped in tightly.

Supplies are running thin. I can't do the memory techniques, I can't write, I can't read my manuals. I can't continue to wait here, preparing for something I haven't experienced. If there is no change tomorrow I'll bury these notes and walk into the town, venture into the unknown alone. If it means the end of my memory again, my knowledge of myself, it will be a small loss.

Last week I visited a friend of mine. I've visited her a few times over the years. She lives in a home for the harmlessly mad, and I never understand why she's there but she tells me it's necessary.

'I wouldn't survive in the world any more,' she says. 'It can be painful to be reminded of who you are.'

My friend has a long hyphenated name, an ex-husband who was once a colleague of mine, a young son in another country. But after reading these notes I know she must be Risa. We have the same memory of meeting, a garden business lunch with her husband, she in a yellow summer dress, me sweating in my tie. But we don't trust that memory. We know we're friends, just not exactly why, and meet out of a vague fear that once you've linked your destiny with certain people you neglect them at your own peril. The spaces in our memories are so vast we know we must have been collaborators. By bringing us closer to the answer of who we were – are – these notes could be very dangerous.

For work and life I make up a past. Or I have memories but no longer believe them. The red train running around my room is missing. There is no silver science prize. I play myself into my own fiction, creating a hometown, an emigration, an education, career. Only with Risa can I try to reconfigure things. We don't get very far, and we never try very hard. Something in us tells us we live precariously, that under the ease of our lives is a struggle best subdued. We're groping in the realm of shadows for something that will overturn the hegemony of memory.

At our last meeting I told her one of my dreams. It was of a large old wooden house in the forest, and I started to describe it but she knew it better than I did.

'Do you remember Max?' she hissed suddenly.

I recoiled. The house hadn't been a dream but a memory. And a year or two ago I had had another dream. A kiss on the mountain, in the snow.

The following night I dreamed of a view far overlooking the city, where a large rock stood under a cypress. On the weekend I went to find it. The long way came to me easily though I couldn't recall ever having been there – it was a landscape I already knew.

In a metal box two feet under the rock I found these notes – they may have lain there for more than ten years – and decided to extend them by a day before I forget what they are. I know nothing more about the cause, and wouldn't even remember this much without the uneasy images of my sleep. I'll bury them again before the memory is lost, and the notes with it. It's a slow struggle. Is there any other way? And if it is futile, does it really matter, these shards of truth found in the vapours of dreams?

'Was it me?' was my final question for Risa.

She had an answer to a question I didn't entirely understand myself, and shook her head.

'You couldn't regain your past without belief in your own commitment, and that was something we didn't anticipate.'

'I was too weak to overcome doubt?'

'Maybe.'

'Because the most important memory to me was love?'

'Your memory was shaky even in that. You mistook the object of your love.'

'You mean it wasn't Em?'

Risa shook her head, then closed her eyes for a moment. When she opened them, they were watery.

'We were betrayed,' she said, voice breaking. 'But it wasn't by you.'

Now I'm torn between delving into the root of a cause the notes couldn't remind me of, or letting it go. Our efforts before went unrewarded, like those of others who must have tried. Were the collective energies deficient, or the cause itself – or the enemy simply untouchable?

Risa said bury the notes again. There was a world for which it was worth living and dying, but it died when our memory did, and we aren't the ones for this. Perhaps our future selves have a better chance, our strength drawn from waiting. Or whoever someday reads these notes. Someone not divided by the fear and the attraction of freedom, whom loneliness has taught the truth.

From far away, so far it seems at the beginning of time, I hear the voice of Max borne on a draught, and it's speaking of me. It means everything and it means nothing, but I've already redraped myself in the whiteness of stolen memory, and decided to agree with Risa.

※ ※ ※ ※ ※

# MELAMPUS

Farmers know that geese don't take to shrimp. Feed them grain mixed with shrimp and other meat, and the geese will pick out everything besides the shrimp. Grind the shrimp in for protein and the geese will walk away.

Melampus had servants and land, so most of the peasants considered him rich. His wealth, though, gave him more status than he felt he had earned in life. The property had been inherited and the choice of crops probably successful due to lucky shifts in weather rather than any particular diligence or wisdom. So he took measures to lower himself, working in his fields in planting and harvesting seasons with the workers and using language that treated them as equals. This he considered not humility – it would have been arrogant to call himself humble – but a way not to lose connection with his fellow man since his wife had moved away with a wealthy artisan she said she loved more. He busied himself in his work, hoping that by hauling his own produce through the forest to the market twenty kilometres away in town he could carry away with it his own deep sense of shame.

On one of these excursions he spied two intertwining snakes – beautiful but deadly kraits banded black and yellow – along the trail beneath a sala tree, and stopped not to kill them but watch their lovemaking with a deep pity for his own loneliness. He marked the area so on the return journey he could look for them again.

Two days later Melampus returned in the opposite direction, having sold his rice and vegetables at reasonable prices, then drinking a little too heavily in the inn where he had spent the night. His head still throbbed as he came upon the marks cut into tree trunks by his machete, and he remembered the snakes. Gingerly he stepped off the trail and through the undergrowth, hoping to find them without incurring their wrath – a single bite was usually fatal. One lay not far off, beside a large rock, and Melampus, head aching, recognized its markings as those of a female. She had just shed her skin and could hardly move, her body too pale and sensitive. Man and snake looked at one another without hostility. Soon the husband came along, slithering through the brush and delivering in his teeth a meal of fresh mouse, feeding and caring for his wife as if she bore a grave illness. Melampus returned home greatly impressed by the fidelity inherent in snakes, which set a great example for all creatures.

When the time came again to make the trip to market, Melampus could have sent a servant or two but as before wanted to rid his thoughts and dreams of his wife's departure, wanted again to look upon the snakes whose caring gave him hope for the future. But on the way to town he was only able to find the male snake, who lay alone by the same rock and had also just shed his skin and couldn't move. "The female must be out hunting," Melampus thought, but this trip he had no time to wait and set off for town.

He stayed for two days trying to sell food no one wanted. Supplies had recently been carted in from elsewhere, and his vegetables rotted and finally he had to sell the rice at no profit just so he could go home. In a sour mood he came upon the male snake beside its moulted skin, pale and weak and still alone unable to move. "Where is his wife when she's needed?" Melampus thought bitterly as he continued his journey. Only a few steps farther, however, he found the female snake in the company of a male lover. He stopped in horror and watched their acts. The snakes looked conniving, and when both slithered towards the husband Melampus was sure they had evil intentions: the female must have instructed her lover to kill her weak husband because he slunk towards the unknowing snake with an ungraceful trepidation that betrayed the fact he acted under compulsion. Melampus in his mind blended the treachery of this lover with that of the artisan – once a friend of his – who had borne away his wife, and in fury he threw a large rock with all his force at the male snake coming to kill his helpless rival. However, Melampus's aim, guided by anger, was poor, and the rock crushed the head of the female some yards off. The terrified lover slithered away, and Melampus continued home under a new weariness.

The husband from his bed beside the rock had heard noises but wasn't strong enough to investigate. After moulting, something he had eaten had made him ill. He preferred to wait for his wife, who as evening approached still had not shown. Well aware of the dangers of the woods, his thoughts were filled with dread, and he spent a sleepless night of worry and hunger. In the morning light he found his wife's lifeless body with its crushed head not far away, already being attacked by insects and forest rodents. "It was that rich man!" the snake knew, sniffing at the tracks, and vowed to track the scent to its source and kill the murderer. Vengeance was the least he could offer the memory of his poor dear wife, who would never have threatened a human and must have been killed for no reason other than the sport of it.

Despite the sensitivity in his new skin and the uneasiness in his stomach, the krait, sniffing at the tracks in sorrow and rage, followed the trail all the way to the village of the rich man. He hid beneath the man's house, waiting for darkness to cloak him so he could slither inside and lodge his fangs in the sleeping man's neck. He could hear his victim now, talking to a servant.

"You should have seen it," said Melampus in disgust. "A snake, helpless after moulting, waiting for his wife to bring him some food, and she's cavorting with a lover the entire time, goading him into killing her husband while he's still defenceless. It's enough to make a man weep at the treachery of all females!"

His house servant, a young woman with broad shoulders and crooked teeth, was silently pouring tea for him, trying to show interest while hiding her offence at the generalization. She even suspected her master's interpretation of what he had seen might be tainted by his feelings of loss and betrayal, which lurked just beneath the surface of all his voiced observations.

"I don't mean you, Chandara, of course," said Melampus. "I know men can be far more cruel. Women just can't help the treachery that nature dictates to them. I tried to kill the lover snake before he killed the husband, thinking the female might then return to him, but some other force guided my hand and I killed the one more deserving of that rock."

Hearing all this from beneath the house, the snake was shocked. He had never suspected his wife of betraying him. But in retrospect it began to make sense – the absences and the silences and her growing indifference to his love. Then the meat she had brought that made him ill. The sounds of flirtatious laughter in the forest, the tracks of another snake in the dirt. And the man he had come here to kill had in fact been the one who had saved his life! "I will thank him in a way befitting a true friend," he thought grimly.

That night the snake entered the house through a hole in the floorboards. Spying the sleeping Melampus on his cot, he slithered closer without sound, past the hand that had struck down his wife, past the vulnerable neck, until he reached the rich man's head. Silently he extended his forked tongue and rubbed it around the inner part of the man's ear.

Melampus awoke with a start. Seeing the venomous krait before his eyes like the female lizard monster of his dreams, he jumped out of bed and ran screaming from the room.

Chandara, hearing the noise, hurried in from the neighbouring hut where she slept to find her master in a state of agitation.

"Sn ... ake ..." he was saying, breathing through a shuddering panic. "Come to take revenge! Come to kill me for killing his wife!"

Chandara looked at him with concern. "Look at the stupid ugly farmer making such a commotion, waking up the whole district for nothing!"

Melampus was shocked at Chandara's insolence. About to give her a thrashing, he wondered if it wasn't her voice that had spoken. He whirled around but saw nothing.

"I'm sure the snake is gone now," Chandara reassured after checking every room in the house. "It must have come in by accident."

Other servants came to the door from other areas of the property but she waved them back home, saying, "Just a snake."

"Check out these two, master and servant, conniving like a pair of lovers."

Again Melampus darted his eyes around in the curves and shadows of the house for the source of such insolence, but saw nothing that could have uttered those words. Only a pair of swallows high in the rafters looked down at the two of them. Suddenly it dawned on him that the snake might have licked into his right ear the power of understanding the speech of birds. "Is that his revenge?" he wondered doubtfully.

"I think you're imagining vengeance," said Chandara. "Animals don't feel as tied to their partners as we do."

"Is that a declaration of love, or what?" spoke one of the swallows.

"If I ever heard one," said the other. "She's obviously fallen for him."

To Chandara Melampus pointed out the two birds in the rafters. "That's where you're wrong," he said. "Just look at those two. They are a loving couple as much as any human husband and wife."

After a minute of uncomfortable silence he added, "If I haven't gone mad, I think I can understand what they're saying."

"Oh? And what are they saying?" Chandara humoured him.

Melampus was too embarrassed to answer, and Chandara felt it was time to take her leave, before other servants started spreading false rumour. "Will you be all right, then, for the rest of the night?"

Melampus hesitated. "I'm still afraid. Would you mind staying?"


To banish the gossip they announced their engagement at the end of the month, Melampus feeling what good fortune it was that his wife had left him, and Chandara a mild embarrassment and grim happiness that her life situation could be reversed through such a simple stroke of love. Melampus felt more content now to settle into his role as rich man, though he continued to make an effort with harvesting and planting, and now and then during a domestic tension still carted produce to market by himself. After their marriage Chandara was rewarded for her years of good service with a servant of her own, and along with the occasional useless but glittering craft brought back from town this kept her content most of the time. Melampus could still understand the speech of feathered animals, though usually this consisted of much of the same banalities as did the speech of humans. But this power had helped win him a wife and dispel his loneliness, and he was grateful. He kept hoping to run across the snake to thank it for this gift, but it never appeared again.

Once on a trip back from market two robbers jumped him from the sides of the path. They quickly bound him and took his money.

As they were leading him into the bushes to cut his throat he heard two birds warning each other about a large decayed branch that was about to fall from its dead tree. "No, that creaking one, over there," a bird instructed to another. Melampus led the robbers under the spot and paused, so that the branch struck them as it fell. As the dazed robbers freed themselves from its weight Melampus undid his binds and fled. The men hurried after him, slicing at the air behind him with their machetes, but he heard another warning from above and circled a cobra grove, into which the robbers bounded with murderous zeal. The snakes felled each with a single strike, continuing until the two men were dead.

Melampus retrieved his stolen money, again grateful for this strange power which had saved him.


During the dry season, hearing that a neighbouring village was slowly expanding, he went to secure the periphery of his property by demarking it more clearly. He came upon a hut technically situated on part of his land, but seeing the nice old couple living there he had no objection. Happy at the honour of having such a rich visitor, they opened their doors to him and since it was already late afternoon persuaded him into staying the night before making the long journey back to his house. Their humility and generosity didn't impress him as much as the fact that their love for each other even after so many years still seemed so strong.

Though it was beyond their means, they fed him a dinner fit for a rich man, and Melampus went to sleep weary and content. The old couple, meanwhile, sat awake concerned about breakfast. What could they prepare in the morning for such an important man? "We have nothing left but the two geese," said the old man. "It's our duty to part with at least one of them after these years." The old woman agreed, and they went to sleep while the two geese beneath the house, having heard all, felt the blood rush to their heads and could hardly speak for anxiety.

"My dear, all is lost!" cried the male goose, stamping his webbed feet in the dirt. "But if our keepers will spare you I will gladly go into the cauldron."

"Let me go!" cried his partner. "Life means nothing to me without you!"

"Nor mine without you. If we must go, let us go together!"

Melampus, roused from his slumber by the commotion, followed the conversation rather touched by the love in animals, as precious as that between humans. In the morning he rose early and entered the kitchen, where the old couple were already preparing a fire. "What is for breakfast?" he asked them, and the old man wagged a finger and said, "That is not for guests to worry about. Go back to bed and rest before your long journey to your home and your wife."

But Melampus persisted and said that the geese must not be harmed, their love as precious as gold, and as he said this he heard the cries of a shrimp merchant outside coming from the village, and he rushed to buy some for their breakfast.

And that is why geese still show respect for what caused them to be spared, once a long time ago, through the virtues of love.

❊ ❊ ❊ ❊ ❊

# BENGALI BLUES

## I

I sit in a Darjeeling guest house and need a subject for my story. It's winter, mist climbing up the mountains, obscuring the views by day and curling into the rooms at night. The place is nearly empty. The Austrian who arrived today will have to do. He seems distracted, a bit down. I'll give him a nice Korean girl to love, or an Israeli, since the travellers around here all seem to be Koreans and Israelis. To make the love story as heavy as his demeanour, there should be a final farewell looming. We'll place the two of them in an airport in a dirty hot city, not too far away. Let's say it's Kolkata. Or Delhi, or even Bangkok. But they met somewhere else, a few weeks ago, in a lakeside town surrounded by Himalayan peaks. Pokhara in Nepal?

So they were in Pokhara a month ago when he fell in love with her, before she left him behind to continue on her travels, and soon they'll be at the airport in Kolkata because she's flying home to Seoul (Tel Aviv?), but wanted to see him one last time.

They haven't even kissed. Their romance, if you can call it that, centres on him professing his love and her verbal and psychological abuse of him. At least that's how he sees it.

Tobias Poos, when he first met Eun-young, wasn't impressed. There was Sara, a French-Swiss twenty-five-year-old in the Pokhara Lakeview

Inn he thought was beautiful, at ease with the world and her place in it. And the Korean he considered a bit ditzy, still young and unformed. Her English wasn't great. She wore loose linen and cotton clothes in colours or styles that didn't match. She would come by his room to show her disjointed sketches of locals and sights and disappear when he joked they were borderline psychotic. He asked her to join him for lunch and she said she had to wash her hair, then showed up an hour later, hair unwashed. They went out for drinks one night with Sara and Ari, an American-Israeli who divided his time between New York and Haifa. Tobias taught her lover's German and Ari taught her fighting English. Tobias said, "Noch ein Bierchen, Liebling?" and she said in a small voice, "I'm not your fucking Liebling or your Schatzi, asswipe!" and they all laughed.

Later on the hotel balcony, after everyone had gone to sleep, the two of them stood smoking, looking into the star-sprinkled night reflected in the lake.

"Where you from Germany?" she said.

"Not Germany. Austria. Graz. That's where Arnold Schwarzenegger's from."

"Oh," she answered, looking at him with interest until he added the town didn't really care for its most famous son.

In the ensuing lasting silence, from nowhere, for no reason, love came on him like a punch in the stomach. The sheer force of it winded him. His mind swirled and he looked off the balcony to catch his breath. Colours were vivid, beauty poignant, the darkness contained so much light and colour, fine threads of silk that wound and bound, thick enough to suffocate.

He tried to take her hand. She said, "I have to sleep now," and left him alone on the balcony, his large hand empty, fingers curling around the cold.

In the morning they ran into each other in the restaurant. She said with a smile, "Guten Morgen, Herr Poos," and he answered, "Annyeonghaseyo." She ate her toast, drank her tea and went out without another word. Tobias would have followed, but Ari sat across from him, with great intensity talking of literature and, accusatorily, of the Holocaust. Tobias, mind elsewhere, couldn't extricate himself.

He knew he wasn't her type and tried to imagine who was. She'd probably be drawn to someone young, successful or wearing a clean shirt, hair gelled crisp over the ears, who grew a little facial stubble but wasn't too muscular, who had a lot of friends and placed himself in the centre of their social circles, someone whose strength she could lean against in times of personal crisis and someone she could mother when she felt strong. Someone who would give her a lot of attention but also space, who wouldn't quiz her on every absence or jealously hunt down her missing hours. Perhaps she might find someone like that but more likely she wouldn't, and he already knew she'd make many mistakes, being used by those who didn't love her and using those who loved her – only to cast them aside for someone less loving. She would be drawn to attention and popularity and be repelled by purity of love. She had a low opinion of men, of life, and didn't believe in love. All of this would cause her pain. Even if she accepted his love, he thought grimly, she might never be happy.

No, that was too dismal a thought – he saw the two of them instead in fifty years telling their grandchildren it almost didn't work out, that if he hadn't pursued her from Pokhara to India she never would have realized she needed him. This life of happiness, he'd tell his granddaughter, if not for the power of love could almost have missed them. And Eun-young, seventy-one and still beautiful, would nod and smile and think her twenty-one-year-old self had been a foolish person indeed. While her granddaughter looked up impressed at the power of love.

She could look like a child. Then with a turn of the head, like a woman. Then turn her head and be a child again. She'd had one boyfriend in her life, she said, and only cheated on him with three others. She wanted to experience and experiment more now that she was free. There were monsters in her past but she wouldn't say who they were, what they looked like, what shapes and colours they wore. There are things no one can speak of, she said, too many evils, and all life is pain. As she spoke this with such conviction he wanted to put his arms around her, wanted her to place her head on his shoulder so he could say the future is full of hope.

"This extraordinary view, these wonderful people, there's beauty everywhere. And there's love to give shape and meaning to life."

"No love!" she said fiercely. "It is big lie."

"Then what is there?"

"Only nothing. Only flame. Only dream."

"You're wrong," he said, but he had lost her, she didn't believe what he thought he believed. "Love is the most beautiful power on earth."

But he was in love and miserable. He hoped to force love into her resistance until it broke.

"You'll think back on this time and realize you were happy here. Memory will make you fond of me."

"I forget you. India and Nepal will be nice when I look at pictures, but … like dream. And photos of you mean nothing."

"How can you be sure?"

"Because you mean nothing now. Your hug is nice, but when memory is weak you will be less. There is always someone to hug me."

Whenever he thought Eun-young had fled from him, would never again let him speak to her of love, she would come back for a few minutes at a time, smiling and asking if he really liked her, then disappearing when he nodded. They went drinking again and he tried to kiss her but she said, "Fuck off!"

"I'll keep trying to kiss you."

"I'll hit you, I'll go away. I'll kill you."

He didn't mind a beating from her but was afraid she really would go away, and he'd be left alone with only her fading image. And there was a disturbing element in her sketches of bloodshot-eyed rickshaw drivers, of gaunt beggar women and scarred children, that made him think she was actually capable of murder.

Then in the morning when he woke she had checked out and was gone. He wandered the town, looked up at the Annapurna Range, then down at its reflection in the lake. He had no way to contact her, but she had his email, there was a chance she might think of him and send word.

She didn't. He waited a week, then needed to get out of town to escape the memory of her.

In their conversations she'd mentioned going on to India. So he would go to India, to follow her. The problem was it was an awfully big place. He went directly east, with a Dane who wanted to go halfway up Everest. Tobias continued on into India alone, and the first tourist town past the border was this tea station.

In Darjeeling Tobias stares for forty minutes at a time at a smudge on a tablecloth. He has no appetite, eats listlessly only because it provides an activity. He sips a Tibetan *thukpa* for an hour, two if there's sentimental music playing, and in his state any music is sentimental. He walks through the village and doesn't notice when it rains. He wanders the dirty streets, Nepalese stopping him to sell something, Tibetans to ask questions, but he doesn't know how to answer. When he speaks, it sounds tinny and hollow. His laughter contains a grain of hysteria, the pitch of a madman.

He tries to fill her absence by drinking with me, but every deficit in sobriety only accentuates how little substance he has, that he can fill himself with beer but once it passes the void in him has increased. After he smokes hash and the smoke and the red eyes clear, he sees there is nothing in the world worth seeing unless her eyes are there to share in it, unless he can whisper his impressions to her and she hers to him. He runs out of hash and buys some more on Promontory Hill. He shows it to me, a black and sticky ball with waxy texture and not the smell it should have. I have my doubts but say nothing.

When the flu stuffs him up and there is no one to talk to – there's only me around, and I'm spending most of the day writing his story – how can he not miss her? After three weeks of absence her face still haunts the inner film of his eyelids, her body becomes whatever his hands are holding. His mind is clogged with her image, his memory hurts. Are there blemishes on her face, flaws in her character? Her face might be unbalanced, her character part evil, her soul confused, and it doesn't matter – he'll look past anything if she'll love him. Or even if she won't, if she just lets him love her.

That final day in Pokhara! They walked to Bindhyabasini Temple and hugged until an angry crowd, incensed at their sacrilege, forced them out. They spent time in cafés and talked of past and present and future. And when she left the next morning, at dawn without goodbye, why wasn't that the end of it? Why doesn't the suffering ease as time passes?

He has long considered himself a person of strength. Independent, marked by substance, depth and opinions. Not one to abandon himself to girl or drug, sect or ideology. But she is a new beacon in the expansive dark haze of his life. He's ashamed to admit she could give him a gun and he would probably kill for her, if a bad person from her past was causing her misery. Kill for a smile from her, for more time. Kill for acceptance, slaughter for love.

He doesn't know what to call himself, he is unrecognizable, foreign to himself. Once he thought of her as unformed, green, naive. Now he is the one unforming, unravelling, and she is solidity for him to lean against.

I like Tobias. Ideas grab hold of him and he is their slave. The brown curls of his hair fly in all directions. He has sleepy green eyes that blink and listen. In our few conversations together we strike up a friendship perhaps strong enough to last beyond this trip. Mostly, though, his mind is elsewhere. I don't know how to help him.

Then he gets the email he's been waiting for:

*Now in varanashi, it crazee place! to kalcuta on fryday, will stay at salvashon hotel.*

There is nothing else, but for him it's enough. As he leaves by jeep for Suliguri to catch the overnight train to Kolkata, I tell him to keep in touch. I wish him luck with the girl. At the last comment he starts, then looks at me suspiciously, unable to remember how much of Eun-young he has revealed. I give him a reassuring smile because, after all, most of his story has been inferred.

# II

Black or white Ambassadors or small Toyotas or Tatas drive past, bobbling over potholes. The air is thick and sweltering, and bicycle bells and donkey brays and ice cream jingles decorate the mechanical sounds of the city. There are heavy dark clouds overhead but they move steadily against the blue.

"Why I should like you?" Eun-young says, "when hundred more handsome or interesting men around?"

"I think you do like me," Tobias answers slowly, "and cruelty is your way of showing it."

To this Eun-young laughs. "You more crazy idiot than before!"

Tobias bursts out laughing but chokes it back before bitterness wells. "I think," he says, "after a week back home you'll realize you like me."

On their park bench at the Victoria Memorial, they laugh together at this new absurdity. This time his laughs do turn to tears he has to turn his face away to hide. She doesn't notice, her laughter free and unrestrained, and she feels so good she even lets him place his hand upon her knee, lean towards her and whisper I love you, before shoving him away.

"I leave day after tomorrow," she says.

"You can't!"

"I pay flight. I go home."

"You can change your flight. You can stay."

"Why? I don't like you."

"Maybe someday …"

"I never like you and you never can kiss me."

"I can keep trying."

Later they drink beers in her hotel room. He has only this night and half of tomorrow in Kolkata for imprinting memories, a deadline for creating love, and the time is insufficient, the potential agony too great. He has a hope, though – a glimmer of belief in the power of love.

She catalogues past lovers, sex acts, along with the reasons she can't stand the sight of him. She embellishes, punctuates her statements with profanities in English he's only just taught her. He winces, and gives her a Tibetan knot of eternity in turquoise and silver he brought back from Nepal. She takes it without thanks but calls him crazy Austria lunatic man. He asks her not to board the flight.

"And do what?"

"Stay another month in India with me."

She bursts out laughing. He waits for a different reply because there's nothing else he can do.

He talks of hash in Darjeeling, hallucinogenic bhang lassis in Pushkar, and she seems interested. He asks her if she wants to try. He shows her the waxy ball he bought on Promontory Hill in Darjeeling. She puts it to her nostril, inhales, screws up her nose. And nods. He doesn't have a pipe on him, and the room has a smoke detector. So they divide the black sticky hash and swallow it. They talk and forget. They drink quickly and the alcohol loosens them.

She speaks harsh words through the face of an angel. His overriding compulsion is to hold her close. Because of the alcohol she allows it; she curls herself into a ball and lets him curl his body around her. He is like someone dying in the desert who stumbles onto an oasis and in a delirium drinks himself to death. His happiness turns to arousal, and she pushes him away from her in disgust.

"Maybe I like girls more."

He shakes his head. "You're too flattered by men's interest."

"Not by you. Don't push your thing at me."

An hour later they've realized the hash is no good. She turns paler than moonlight. His mind is a hive of doubt, fears, horrors – he starts cradling himself, rocking the horror to go away. From the bathroom comes the sound of her retching. He is already praying for the day to come.

In his mind are no monsters or snakes, only one frantic thought leading to the next. A labyrinth in which he roams and soon is lost – with the pervading fear he'll never recover, that when the drug wears off his mind will be lost roaming the labyrinth, prematurely senile and unloved.

The shower has been running for what seems hours but he can't move. He flails out at the thoughts flying through his mind and steadies himself. He steps up to the bathroom door and listens and hears nothing but running water, a drain gurgling. Is she dead? He tries the door but it's locked. He scratches at the door and whispers, "My darling …" To him it sounds creepy. As if he tried to drug her into submission. No wonder she locked herself away. Thoughts heave in him. He has killed her. His love has smothered her. His mind will never again be clear enough to think. These voices and black-hooded notions which have now entered him, at twenty-nine, will never leave. He swears off hash. NEVER AGAIN! he screams at his mind, trying to imprint this command with enough ferocity for its mandate to last beyond the night.

He pounds at the door. "Are you OK?" he whispers through clenched teeth. There is no sound but water. "Eun-young!" he says shrilly, and it's almost a scream. To his relief he hears the sound of retching again. The shower stops. The door opens. She is in her clothes, dripping wet. Her skin is so pale he can almost see through it. Eyes barely open.

"You OK?"

She shakes her head. He wants to hold her, will away her pain, but she points to the far door. "Go."

He retreats a few paces and looks back. Her arms around the toilet bowl, she has closed her eyes again. She might need him, he can't leave, she could die in the night. He lies down on the bed and wills time to move more quickly and heal her. But his mind is a swarm of bees in the windowless room. If he lies still his thoughts and breathing spin and fly. He returns to the girl and, afraid to wake her, kisses the air beside her neck. He slides one arm under her knees, another behind her wet back and lifts her. She's light – no wonder her body can't digest the hash. He carries her to the bed, wondering if it's best to remove her wet clothes. She opens her eyes and they're fearful and angry.

"I'm sorry," he whispers.

She mumbles something he can't catch. He places his ear above her mouth and makes out the words "fucker" and "go". He retreats to the other edge of the bed. With great force of will she hauls her body up and back into the bathroom. The door locks. The sound of retching. Again the endless stream of the shower.

Please! he begs of God, let this pass. Let it be morning.

In the windowless hotel room, though, there is no light, no movement in time, only a girl and himself both being killed by his love.

After a night like this nothing is the same. The girl you love looks at you differently. The terror has placed so much pressure on your brain it now functions differently. It's slower, thought comes in frames of images. His mind, from suffering and the lingering bhang, isn't clear. He turns off the light and closes his eyes, but she's inescapable, he can't shut her out, can't close himself to her. Part of him has become her image, he exists only as far as he exists for her, which isn't enough. He's afraid of the balcony – the wondering if he might leap. As if there were two of him, and each can't be trusted – ready to murder the other in the assumption it might liberate the survivor.

On the final day she goes shopping for jeans and souvenirs and leaves him for an hour. He lies face down on the bed, banging his head into the sheets to drive love out of him. When she flies he'll be an empty shell. And in her mind she's already gone; she has told him they won't meet again. And he can't – for the sake of his sanity – believe her, he holds her image in a suffocating embrace. Their romance was always a race against time, a few days in Pokhara, two days in Kolkata, to make her love him. Now the clock has wound down. When she returns from final souvenir shopping they'll have a few final minutes, but he has failed. A few minutes won't change anything.

He has her bags, and thinks of stealing her passport from her carry-on. She'll only hate him more, though, not surrender.

It's the waiting, the not being with her, the inability to go out. Action is denied him; nothing to do but hope for the possibility of her.

When she walks in the door he says, "*Sa rang hae yo.*"

"I don't love you," she answers.

"Why did you send me an email, if you hate me so much? You knew I'd come."

"Yesterday my birthday." She grimaces. "I want hug."

"Happy birthday."

He leans over and kisses her on the mouth. She lets him but doesn't kiss back.

"You can't do that."

"Why do you always push me away?"

"Because you don't hear what I say."

He hugs her stiff body and his eyes turn liquid.

"We never meet again," she whispers. "You write me I don't answer."

She refuses to let him come to the airport. He hops into her taxi anyway. For a moment she says nothing, he thinks he has won her acquiescence, but two kilometres down the road she tells the driver to stop and Tobias to get the fuck out.

Wandering dirty streets, he feels he'll never be as strong as he was before he met her, a girl he has known five days in two countries, now leaving him forever. Five days! What sort of love can come out of that? Why can't he shut it off, drink it away or purge it with antibiotics like a bout of Delhi diarrhoea?

What he always thought of as sentimentality in song or literature, he now lives. The loss that drives you to madness or suicide. He wonders if these fates await him. How much time does he have left as himself? Or has the person he thought himself to be already died?

He leans his head back and opens his mouth and laughs, a choking laugh that threatens to turn to sobs. Then he wants to weep but can't. Tears might help purge her ghost from his mind, but he can't escape her haunting.

He flags down the next taxi. "To the airport!" he says without haggling. The driver smiles with a circular nod. Along the way it occurs to Tobias he'll be charged something extortionate. "Quick!" is the only thing he utters.

It's a small airport and those without tickets can't enter the departure lobby. His mind isn't working – it takes him twenty minutes of pacing the pavement in a whirl of confusion to remember that baksheesh opens doors. Five hundred rupees gets him through, but it's too late – only some Indian businessmen and a Japanese in a hippie dress stand in the check-in line. He has vacillated too long, Eun-young has passed through the immigration doors.

When he has hold over himself he tries to find a window, to spot her plane among others waiting to depart, but sees nothing. He finds a better window. A few take off; he doesn't know which machine is flying her away from him. Only from the board's *AI203 – Seoul, Incheon – Departed*, does he know that she's gone.

His only hope, this love-sick Austrian, now lies with me, with the act of me sitting in misty Darjeeling writing his story. As much as I like Tobias, I'm not sure if I should finish. It could turn out that several years down the road Eun-young will read it, in English or translation, and reconsider the past. She might even contact the author, as a way to pass a note to Tobias. I might then invite her out for coffee, so I can ask her questions, get to know her better. You're a character in my story, I'll say. It's time to get your side of it.

✠ ✠ ✠ ✠ ✠

# BLACK DOG

When I arrived, the one I liked best was Hasegawa Makoto. He stopped me on the first day, a diffident young man who struck me as so grounded that I mistook him for staff. Only on closer observation did I notice he sat hunched over, that the corners of his eyes shifted, that he spoke with vaguely slurred speech as if he had once had a stroke, but quickly, easily losing the thread of the conversation.

"You the new doctor?"

"Just someone to change things around here a little, add ideas, expand treatments."

He cocked his head as I spoke, then chuckled. "You have your work cut out for you. Adding ideas …" But he lost the idea, screwed up his eyes, then dismissed me by returning to his book, a novel by Dazai.

The patients here are not the category of mentally disturbed who need tranquilizers and padded walls, who howl through the night in their restraints. They suffer from neuroses and phobias and depression. Many checked in voluntarily knowing they have problems and could leave if they wanted to. Few have made a complete recovery through treatment so they stay on out of habit and the growing belief that they would fit in nowhere else. The staff tell them their daily schedule, advising on choice of music, books to read, even cutting their meat into small pieces for them and telling them to eat more rice.

Those with authority in my country (doctors, teachers, lawmakers) too often try to regiment the lives of those without. The first thing I felt I had to change in the clinic was to make the patients more resourceful, give them some responsibility over their own well-being, raise their level of expectations. As Professor Heilbutt in Lucerne taught me, it is amazing how much progress can be made when the burden falls collectively. So I began doing my rounds, introducing myself and getting to know the residents.

When I saw Makoto again the next day, he paced the common room looking more animated. Then he would stop pacing, sit down and with his face just a foot from the page scribble furiously in a little tattered black book, then just as suddenly stand up and start pacing again, arms and hands describing small arcs, mind working through some riddle he had posed of himself. To calm him down I asked him why he thought he was here.

"What do you think?" he replied with one raised eyebrow and a smirk.

I admitted I had read his file, which mentioned a mild hebephrenic schizophrenia, and decided to be honest with him. "It was recommended by a specialist in the capital because of delusions, paranoia, erratic behaviour, occasional violence."

He started to laugh and say something but I cut him off. "I know full well that three-quarters of psychiatric patients in this country are misdiagnosed. What do *you* understand as your reasons for being here?"

He pondered for a minute or two. Finally he straightened his posture. "There's no such thing" – he held up an extended finger as if launching into something rehearsed – "as understanding. It's too complex. But we here know what we don't know, we understand the world is illusory and everyone in it is consumed by the illusion – and *that* is the difference between the mad and the others, who walk on a knife-edge but have no idea."

A word like mad can be unhelpful if it aggravates a stigma, and is to be discouraged. "What about patients like your neighbour Ken?" I pointed out nevertheless. "Does he understand better than others the illusory nature of life? – He thinks he's God!"

"He's just a fool."

Talking patients out of their phobias and grandiose concepts can be one of the most effective avenues of treatment. It is the theory of Professor Heilbutt, reigning expert in psychiatric treatment in Lucerne, that you have to examine each case on an individual basis. Only after understanding the history and nature of the problem can you advise on a social programme or course of treatment. This is why my work takes time, and why some of my colleagues in this country consider it invasive and wasteful. But to me it makes perfect sense. An older patient here, Takahara Yasu, for example, believes that for the sake of future peace and prosperity eccentrics should inherit the earth – but he is an eccentric so such a belief would follow naturally. Another is a conspiracy theorist who spends his time on the internet researching clans, clubs and elitist conferences, freemasons, the Vatican and international royalty such as our beloved emperor, Rockefellers and Rothschilds, secret services of various governments and organized crime. Because Jo Masayuki's view is that when he points out connections among these groups he is considered absurd – and if existence itself is absurd then what counts as absurdity within the absurd must be truth! Logic such as this shouldn't be too difficult to discredit, given enough time. And no matter how much evidence he thinks he unearths and shows me, it will never prove an argument which is inherently flawed.

"You just said that those here understand more of what they don't know than those outside," I continued.

"If you believe that … it only proves my point – you know less than you think you do!"

"I didn't say I believed it."

"You used it against me in order to prove your own ignorance."

"You're the one who's changing your argument!"

"My argument is the same, only you've bent it to fit your own warped reason!"

"If your argument were constant I couldn't be using your own contradictions against you."

"Exactly! You just proved my point."

"What point?"

"That your conventional explanations don't hold up. You might as well be here instead of me!"

Our discussions continued regularly like this in the ensuing week, and I enjoyed the exchanges even though Makoto, in his illogical way, often thought he had outwitted me. Patients never responded with such complexity in Europe. Dr Igarashi looked on at my methods with something resembling disdain. Nurse Gomibuchi wouldn't have cared what I tried, as long as I didn't make the job any more difficult for her by upsetting the patients. Of that, despite everything that has happened, I had no intention.

Annually for ten years now, in my country between thirty and forty thousand people – overworked businessmen, bullied schoolchildren, the chronically ill, the suddenly unemployed – decide not only that life is no longer worth living but are successful in their attempt to end it. And my country has few guns, so people must be determined or creative in their suicides. They jump from buildings, in front of trains on the Yamanote Line, into the crater at Oshima or into Lake Biwa with a lover, siphon carbon monoxide back into their cars, swallow vials of Ambien, hang themselves with plastic twine intended for recyclables, even disembowel themselves with a kitchen knife. Those without that imagination or fortitude wallow in their melancholy (SSRIs are hard to get, and depression so stigmatized few consider seeking help, or consider it helpful when they do), retreat from society (some families leave food at the bedroom door for a son they live with but haven't seen in years), or enter one of sixteen hundred brimming clinics that lack doctors trained to deal with them.

The Ministry of Health finally began to acknowledge the problem, and sent me – with most of my education admittedly theoretical, not yet applied – to one of its mental health clinics in the mountains to advise the local staff on courses of treatment. As a specialist who studied methodology in Hungary, Finland, Switzerland – countries rich in depression and mental illness – to supplement doctoral research at St John's College, Cambridge, I'd like to think I can help right this sinking ship.

With high hopes of validating Professor Heilbutt's theories I arrived a month ago. The clinic here, with a euphemistic name similar to View of the Snow Country, is run by the bespectacled Igarashi Genki. No one takes kindly to being told how to do his job, so the lack of eye contact or bow on my reception was expected. Igarashi has the red podgy nose of an alcoholic, and his pockmarked face flakes with a recurring skin condition. Despite the alpine climate, he sweats easily and suffers from chronic shortness of breath. Short arms flop around as he speaks, which can make him look like an erratic penguin. Which is deceiving; he can betray a profound cunning or a sudden fit of violence (more on that later). Despite reigning like a king in an isolated kingdom, he follows and enforces the rules fairly responsibly, even when the rules make no sense.

The head nurse, Gomibuchi Makiko, is a fifty-year-old woman with caking make-up and a shrugging fatalism, like a former sex worker.

She says words like "indeed" or "actually" far too often, followed by something inconsequential that never needed an "indeed" or an "actually". She wears a beige nurse's uniform every day, her wavy hair tied up, with the same house shoes and same skin-tone stockings and same resigned expression so that she no longer seems very real to me, more like a box which, when opened, continues the same tune it stopped when you closed it last time.

There is also another part-time doctor, a male nurse who doubles as a guard, three female nurses of varying ages who double as cleaners or cooks, an additional weekend guard and a permanent gardener/ guard, who seems to do little more than drink whisky and sit around the property. Most of them were recruited from the village five kilometres away and in the evening return there to their families. Once a fortnight someone from the prefectural office comes to make sure the subsidies are sufficient for food and supplies. A psychiatrist from the capital joins him a few times a year. We have thirty-five resident patients, which is well under the two-hundred-plus national average, and all have been here several years, so I suspect Igarashi has a friendly contact within the Ministry of Health who could close the clinic to new patients. Few visitors come, and only on Sundays. I was sent to this particular clinic, I imagine, because of its isolation and state of stasis, so that if there are benefits from my treatments they will be easy to analyse. Another reason may be the fact that five patients here – all women – took their own lives in the past seven years.

In the women's section of the large rhombus-shaped building lives a city girl named Tanigawa Shiori. She is a veritable doll – thin, twenty-four, with disproportionately thick legs but delicate pale features and a small head with long hair and a sharply defined chin. Seen from a distance you could mistake her for a work of porcelain. Every morning she rises early and spends an hour on her make-up, which she applies so subtly – a touch of rouge here, a slight shading there – that the less observant wouldn't notice it. She speaks softly in a high voice, almost a whisper, that you have to bring your ear close to her mouth as she speaks. This proximity scares her into pulling away, looking down and speaking even more quietly, so that you have to go away and try again later.

Her delicate appearance masks a strong will, and Nurse Gomibuchi has reported of Shiori refusing medicine or morning exercise on some of her many moody days. Though communication is difficult, Shiori is one of only three patients here with any kind of university degree. She studied French existentialism in the capital, at the best university in the country. Her dissertation on Sartre's *Being and Nothingness* was archived on the university website and I read it a week ago – fifty intricate and persuasive pages. Despite her literate rationality, though, I think she is in love with Makoto. Her eyes follow him at meals; when he speaks either genuine wisdom or utter nonsense she blinks at him as if his words were absolute. But I suppose there are not many other men around here one could love.

Of Igarashi she seems terrified, going the other way when he approaches. I asked her about this but she looked away and mumbled something. For any sensitive young woman, I suppose such a fleshy, wheezing, myopic character would only be frightening.


About one week into my visit I did something I'm not proud of, and which began the series of problems that followed. Many patients were out walking in the garden. Makoto's little book lay on the table where he'd left it in his haste to get outside and pace the flower bed. I took a quick peek at its tattered pages, mainly to see if in writing he could follow the linearity he lacked in speech. He couldn't, seeming lost in labyrinths of point and counter-point. He would scribble *Anyone who thinks Mozart or Kawabata is no genius is a fool!* then follow it up with *There's no such thing as genius – any fool knows that!* Rambling on at the absence of absolutes, the presence only of hypocrisy, he'd conclude: *And all this is what is called life. What a farce!*

But on one page in the middle, something I saw made me stop. *Sleeping with a girl is the easy part*, he had written in very quick, poorly legible pencil. *They're the ones who do the seducing – and the best deny they're capable of such things, which just proves that <u>instinct</u> has made them natural seductresses – so in the end you simply have to bed them down. They might say no, or beat at you with their little fists, or cry, but afterwards you can't get rid of them, and they follow you around so that the whole world knows how base you are! And this one – she speaks so you can't even hear, weaving you towards her until you're caught helpless in her circles of existentialism and she can do as she likes with you!*

He could have only been writing of Shiori. Whether he spoke of sex, or even rape, though, wasn't clear, and I felt duty-bound to investigate – for the sake of Shiori, and Makoto, and preserving the fragile calm of the clinic, where in recent years five women had already taken their own lives.

Then I made my second mistake – why did I have to give him this ammunition to aim at me? I went to Igarashi, told him what I'd read, and asked if he knew of any intimacies among patients or hints of sexual violence in Makoto. Igarashi sat unmoving as I spoke, but when I finished he stood up, winced as if overcome by sudden chest pain or nausea – what Professor Heilbutt in another context would have attributed to acute anxiety – and his arms shuddered as his agitation found its expression in anger. For the first time I noticed his fingernails were gnawed, though previously only tobacco dependency and his clammy hands would have counted as evidence of nervousness in him. "You've broken the rules!" he wheezed. "You know you can't rummage through their private possessions!"

Seeking help from this man was a waste of time. I shrugged and turned to go, but he stopped me. "Have you ever worked in a clinic before?"

"Of course, in Lucerne I assisted the great—"

Igarashi drowned me out: "I've worked with patients for twenty-five years! With some of those here for a decade! I know what they respond to. You don't know these kinds of illnesses or these individuals and have no idea how disruptive your approach is!"

"And you," I cut in, "have no imagination, no observation skills, a fixation on rules rather than positive change, intent on ruling a fiefdom where—"

"Let me give you an example. A hundred years ago schizophrenia was a brain disease. Fifty years ago a pseudo-science took root and turned it into a psychological disorder caused by bad parenting! A legion of Freudians started blaming schizophrenogenic mothers and phantom traumas of childhood. Then chlorpromazine arrived to prove it *is* an organic disorder. Without inexperienced theorists running around taking everyone's focus off the real problems we would be farther along in treatment today.

"Now you're doing the same, ruining the stability we've worked years to achieve here! Patients, above everything, need an environment where they feel safe."

I glanced down at my notebook and read off five names: "Uchibori Naoko, Kamijima Futaba, Tai Etsuko, Yamanaka Nami, Abe Shinobu." These were the women whose deaths this man was responsible for, and a fittingly cutting parting shot.

Back in my guest room I tried to update my notes but my mind was too active. An image of Shiori, silent but needing help, floated in and out of my thoughts. Then that of my mother, swinging from the apple tree in full bloom in the yard, amidst the white petals above my six-year-old self. Finally as I lay in bed pondering my misjudgement in confiding in an ignorant buffoon like Igarashi, I drifted into sleep. Later I woke to what I thought might have been a scream and a crash, but remembered a dream that in its dark, lurking dog-like shadows had involved a scream and a crash, and went back to sleep.

In the morning I discovered what had happened. Igarashi had given Makoto one hell of a beating, then stormed off to the village – to drink at the inn for a few days, I assumed. Gomibuchi had dressed Makoto's bruises and cuts, but had no idea what the conflict had been about. "Actually, I wasn't here. Indeed, it's worrying."

Makoto wouldn't speak to me. He had bruises on his face, upper torso and legs, abrasions where he had been hauled along the ground, but according to the nurses no fractures or internal injuries. When I asked him something he turned away from me and trembled, as if with an unfocused, general hatred.

For information I went to see Ogawa Kenichiro, who lives in the neighbouring room. Ken is a megalomaniac, but an endearing one, who thinks he is the only one in the world with consciousness and therefore an omnipotent deity. He never bathes, only lets the nurses sponge him down sometimes, and would never change clothes if it weren't done for him. He prefers long, flowing shirts and robes and combs his hair down over his eyes.

"I can see everything and hear everything," he spoke calmly, nodding his squarish head. "You are here to ask me questions."

"Well, obviously."

"And you know why he was beaten?"

"No."

"I think you do know."

"Why don't you tell me what you heard?"

"I heard you walking outside my room just now, back and forth twice before you knocked."

"Yes."

"You think you might be responsible."

"I don't know."

He ate a piece of chocolate (which at that hour was against Igarashi's rules), and studied his right foot for a moment. "It was about the girl."

"What about Shiori?"

A knowing sigh, eyes narrowing. "They both touch her."

"You're mistaken!"

His expression remained enigmatic, but rather than being insightful or perceptive, his words just seemed like all his words ever did. Speaking little in expansive abstractions – it was his way to feel wise without giving away that he wasn't.


Igarashi returned the next day and to my surprise was entirely sober. Without discussion or apology, the routine simply continued, and I thought it best for my relationship with the staff if I didn't interrupt my examination of the patients. Makoto was still sulking so I thought I would gently press Shiori into disclosing anything about herself. But she interpreted my "Tell me about your father" as criticism of him and, by extension, of her, and spoke so quietly again – right hand incessantly smoothing out her hair, looking at the floor – that listening was pointless. I asked her to speak up, but she looked so chastised that she might burst into tears. Asking her anything of love would have been counterproductive.

When I went to make my disgust at the beating clear with Igarashi, he sat in his office talking on the telephone. Seeing me, he spoke, "Yes, of course. Most strange, of course, disruptive, but more later." As he put the phone down, he looked straight at me, a rare moment of eye contact. "I'm very busy at the moment, as you can see."

"It's rather important. I want to talk about what happened—"

He cut me off in anger. "Because of your violations, he became unruly and lunged at me without provocation! Luckily I could react and defend myself. When patients know their possessions have been searched, their private thoughts screened, it can make them act aggressively. You know that fully well – especially when the patient suffers from paranoia and persecution phobia! He thought I'd been the one spying on him. I didn't tell him the truth, but have made an official complaint with the prefectural office and the Ministry will certainly hear about this!"

And so things had become rather bad. I was sure there was more to all this than my snooping, but I was the one breaking rules and so found myself on the wrong end of virtue. My recommendations on treatments would go nowhere.

The patients are always sensitive to atmosphere and mood and could sense that all was not well in the clinic. My presence, it seemed, had made things worse by upsetting the routine of the staff, and therefore the dull unimaginative peace through which it moves. Even Gomibuchi showed signs of eye-rolling frustration when I asked her for another half hour alone with Jo Masayuki the conspiracy theorist.

And when I entered, Masayuki frowned. I started asking him for information on the five suicides but his eyes widened.

"They're after you!" he spoke.

"Who?"

"They all hate you!"

When I asked for elaboration Masayuki babbled on in his hand-wringing, eye-popping manner on the backroom manipulations behind any government policy in the higher levels, even on how Ministry of Health funds were distributed and how clinics preserved their allocations. I was too tired to argue with him.

Later by fax I received a copy of a report filed with the prefectural office and sent to the Health Ministry. It was Igarashi's list of rule breaches I had committed since arriving. I had taken a patient for a walk outside the garden walls on a weekday for the purpose of holding a private interrogation; I had encouraged another to skip morning exercise, probably for the same reason; I had found one drinking an evening whisky and not confiscated it; I had tried to make meal times more flexible and encouraged certain forbidden hobbies like poker, with the excuse that it might serve as a precursor to group counselling; I had spied among personal belongings and spent the bulk of my time in aimless confrontational conversation with hypersensitive patients. The report concluded I had yet to make any recommendations on treatment, nor was I likely to, that my stay had provoked violence in one patient, extreme social withdrawal in another, as well as general unrest and unease and an epidemic of rule breaches. I was asking *patients* to recommend their own course of treatment, which was more responsibility than any of them were ready for. My methods were a waste of time and money and it was recommended that I be transferred elsewhere or removed from my post.

All quite heavy and I felt demoralized. Shadowy hounds of doubt swarmed over the furniture in the rooms of my mind. I had no ally in the entire clinic. Confronting Igarashi again would be a waste of time, but I needed a defence against his accusations, some evidence my efforts were achieving something. I decided to try my luck again with Makoto.

"Back for more?" These were his first words to me in nearly a week. He looked up from his journal with screwed-up eyes.

"How do you feel?"

He shrugged.

"Igarashi says you tried to attack him."

Makoto laughed and looked away.

"The atmosphere here is no good recently."

He laughed again. His tone was mocking. "Feeling unsure of your methods? That discussion might not be the same thing as cure?"

Never show self-doubt, is another of Professor Heilbutt's tenets. "What do you think is a good way to improve communication and mood here?"

His eyes glinted. The tip of his tongue ran across his upper lip. "We should have a party! We've never had one."

But as I walked away he was laughing again. I couldn't believe that from being the most agreeable patient he had become one of the most difficult. Had I arrived at a bad time or was it really my doing?

His suggestion, though, had merit; a gathering with all residents and staff present might be beneficial. Some patients here for a decade still didn't know the names of some of the others. The gardener didn't even know the names of the nurses. Friendships came, if at all, only in pairs. Considering this was such a small community, the lack of intimacy was astounding.

I told Gomibuchi first. At the end of the week everyone would have dinner together. She raised her eyebrows and I reminded her of my authority; she would inform the staff, I would inform the patients. "Indeed, it's unprecedented," she complained.

Igarashi came to see me almost immediately. His fists clenched and unclenched as he spoke. His glasses rose and sank on his face as its expressions changed. "You don't know these people and have no right!" he spoke with drawn-out composure and noxious halitosis. "Forced socialization can undo years of progress!"

"Nonsense," I said. "It's just dinner. This is exactly what Professor Heilbutt, a leader in the field, would have suggested."

Igarashi muttered something about cultural differences, which is the same argument I've heard a hundred times since returning from Europe armed with fresh and better ideas. That we are a different people. We react to and understand different truths, speak an alternate language of experience. But it's all nonsense! I've travelled enough to know that human nature applies to humans. How easy it is to cower behind differences in order to paint the boundaries of some tenuous notion of self! Differences are the illusion, existing and potential connections the reality.

The party began slowly, hesitant dipping of toes in a cold spring. The gardener, teetering and grinning, was drunk, and I suspected some of the patients and lower nurses as well. There was much silence, many Giaconda smiles, ambiguous expressions. Some were looking at the unimpressive watercolours on the wall – boat scene in grey, hydrangea in bloom – as if they had never seen them before. Ken, in a purple flowing robe, fell asleep at his chair. Makoto was in one of his sullen spells again – disappointing, considering the party was his idea. Although forty-one people sat at the same long table, only one conversation among patients was heard at any one time. When I asked Masayuki, who sat beside me, a question, the voices at the far end stopped and listened. No one made eye contact with me; being singled out for public conversation was too much scrutiny to bear. Finally I asked a general question to all: could each of you give a brief self-introduction?

No answer but a contemptuous chuckle from Igarashi. I began by giving a brief summary of my travels and studies. I asked Makoto, then Masayuki, to follow suit, but they only grinned nervously. The gardener gradually leaned to one side in his chair, righting himself at the last moment before falling. Finally a serene, empathetic woman of forty-three named Satsuki took pity on the situation and gave her name and home prefecture. I asked a few questions and bravely she spoke of her last time outside the walls, five years ago. Even the gardener listened.

She had been a translator for an American brokerage firm, but after a while couldn't distinguish the languages any more; what she wrote looked entirely strange to her – it was all sentences without meaning. And then she also stopped being able to translate the objects in her life. Food was too strange to touch, much less eat, and after the first bite every single thing tasted the same. And every person she saw seemed an extension of every other person. People might look a little different, but it was mere deception, since they were the same. She became everyone else, because when they looked at her, or talked to her, it forced a predictable reaction, and that just proved she had no will, no consciousness separate from anyone else. Children on the street tried to play with her, because she acted as if they were her. Most bewildering, and later terrifying, was looking at herself in the mirror, because the face wasn't any*one*, it was just a thing like anything else, a shell of a something. So to a friend she whispered for help, and the friend told her mother and together they found this place, which had helped her start sorting people a little, and where tasting differences in the food didn't really matter since it *was* all the same.

This created a murmur of a laugh and even Shiori smiled. The smile brought some natural colour back to her features. I looked over at

Igarashi, but he was whispering something to Gomibuchi, who looked at me sceptically. Makoto looked over at Igarashi. There seemed some complicity among them.

Dinner was becoming a promising sort of discussion group; after being whispered to by Makoto, another young patient named Yu also opened up and told of his experiences in the outside world. He had kept having horrible, visual prophesies that went unfulfilled. When his mother dropped him off for swimming lessons, her last wave seemed weighted with all the force of doom, and as she drove away he knew, tears flowing, that she would die in a car accident – crash headlong amidst rain and darkness and screaming brakes into a massive truck – and he would never see her again. Two hours later, though, she reappeared, smiling, still very much alive. When his younger brother for an international science competition flew for the first time, Yu also knew it would be his last. He had seen a crow circling the house that morning, which could only mean the worst: the plane would explode mid-ocean once the crow landed. But the next day his brother called from the other side of the Pacific, happily describing how big the cars were there. Or when Yu woke in the morning and the first thing he saw was a fly on the far wall, he remembered a dream and knew it would be the final morning – something disastrous would happen before the next. It never did. Every day was accompanied by presentiments of catastrophe. How could he live in such constant terror? When he had entered this facility, the prophecies became less frequent, the omens less disturbing. At least, until I had come along. As soon as he'd seen me he knew that some disaster would befall them, that he would never be cured and one day suffer a horrible death just as he would foretell it.

His story wound down but any levity created earlier was now gone. Dinner finished tensely and quietly, and Yu felt responsible for the change in mood; he looked nervous to the point of panic.

Makoto raised a hand. He pointed to the end of the table at Tabata Shingo, a patient I had never been able to get a word out of. "Tabata's father and grandfather are the same person," he said with a laugh. "That's what happens in villages that get snowed in all winter like this one!"

The rest of the room went silent, except for the sounds of people shifting in their chairs, looking at the table, inching their toes to the side in order to leave quickly once dismissed. I conceded defeat and said all were free to go if they wanted. All went.

The next day when I tried to talk to him about the dinner, Makoto became aggravated, and two nurses as well as Gomibuchi tried to calm him down without resorting to the haloperidol. He wrote furiously in his little book, then screeched at the top of his lungs, then spoke lucidly on the utter absence of clarity, then flirted with the youngest nurse. I tried to glance casually at his open book on the table but he closed it immediately.

"You'll see," was all he said to me. By then he spoke calmly, though his eyes were wide and his lower teeth closed in front of his upper.

For some reason, Makoto's smile through this jutting jaw hit me with all the weight of paranoia. Were they plotting something against me? What had he written in his little book? It might shed light on the fight with Igarashi, the relationship with Shiori, the recent deaths or the underlying, silently incubating cancer which was affecting the entire clinic. Another of Igarashi's accusations, if anyone caught my sleuthing, would end my career at its beginning. Any rule breaches now would have to be untraceable.

Two days later when the nurses weren't looking I substituted one of Makoto's prescribed neuroleptics with chlordiazepoxide. Combined with his daily lorazepam it would be enough to put him to sleep for a while.

After an hour or so of paperwork I returned. Makoto was sleeping peacefully. I took the book, thumbed through it quietly to find a few pages blacked out and illegible. I began reading from the most recent entry.

*Nothing is absolute*, he wrote. *Nothing you can say can't be refuted! Beethoven is discordant noise to some. For some beings, air is water. Nothing is big because there is always BIGGER! A sphere at a microscopic level, or in the dark, might as well be a cube. There are only degrees, scales, levels of muchness, but then even that's nonsense. At no point can you point at something and say this is. Because from another perspective, maybe it isn't.*

*And you can't give someone a pill and say Now he will sleep, because maybe he won't, maybe the pill will go under the tongue to be spat back out into the sink, and he will lie with eyes closed waiting to catch your red hands break his trust. Because there are rules against such things, even laws. You hold these laws against us, to show why we are on opposite ends of the sanity divide, but now I'm using them against you to prove the divide is inverted.*

It was a direct message to me. I quickly shut the book. In his corner bed, Makoto lay face up, but I couldn't see if his eyes were open. Not knowing what to do, I sat unmoving as my heart beat noisily.


The following week became a blur. Gomibuchi showed me a decree from the Ministry of Health to leave the clinic, effective immediately. I was too dazed to protest as the gardener stumbled along, guiding me out by the elbow. Once outside the grounds, though, I found my voice again. From my mobile I phoned Igarashi at his office and asked for clarification.

"The list of rule breeches extended beyond the limits of tolerance," he spluttered. "A patient made a signed declaration that you drugged him and went through his possessions with the intent to steal valuables."

Hearing his wheezy, nasal breath lecturing *me* became too much – a rage suddenly towered up. "You set all this up! There's something going on in the clinic you don't want me to know about! If anything happens to Shiori, *anything,* I will kill you! Don't think I won't!"

In a tremble of anger I continued down the long road to the village, from where I could catch a train back to the prefectural capital and lodge my counter-accusations. It was a fine spring day with a fresh breeze and crocuses opening by the roadside, but I was in no mood to enjoy the scenery. A black dog began following me, a mixed-breed creature with droopy ears and long face. If I stopped and turned back, he also paused. Though he trotted at a distance and looked friendly enough, his presence seemed tangible evidence of evil, a portent of misfortune. Stooping for a rock on the path, I looked straight into his eyes as my stomach knotted. His expression seemed to sink at my betrayal of our new companionship, and he let me continue on alone.

About halfway to the village a police car intercepted me. "Come with us, please," spoke a young officer with big hands and thin wrists, who sat beside the short driver.

"What's going on?"

A turn of the head indicated I should get in. Once we were moving, the one with large hands turned around and explained.

Igarashi had just phoned them, replaying for them a recording of my "death threat" and claiming he feared for his life. My ill-treatment of patients, he had told them, was evidence enough of my dangerous unpredictability.

Clutching my briefcase, I sat soberly trying to piece together the events of the past weeks, but when we arrived at the police station I held nothing back, let them all know what I thought. I shouted that it was *absurd*, Igarashi was a cunning liar, I'd been set up and they were fools to believe him! Everywhere you looked was only moral weakness, cowardice and lies!

Until an officer took me aside. My shouting, he told me calmly, was far more damaging to my credibility than Igarashi's phone call. They believed there was just some misunderstanding, that I wasn't intent on murder but the local police had been accused last year of negligence in an ill-fated stalking case and couldn't take any chances. They would keep me under surveillance until I calmed down and tomorrow put me on the train to the capital.

Which, after a demoralizing night incarcerated without charges, is what happened. I came home. Based on the "evidence", I was relieved of my position at the Ministry and found myself unemployed and discredited. Worse than this, and the nationwide blacklisting I knew I'd received, was that I was assailed on all sides by a horrific, relentless doubt. This was so thick yesterday I couldn't even cook dinner. The permutations of chance were too horrible and I couldn't continue – what if … and if … and then … could … Every action leading to another was irrevocable, and what if cooking dinner was the wrong path, the one not meant to happen, and I had lost the only chance I would ever have to make things better. Or my studies, travels, career choice … Maybe my beliefs were faulty down to the core and all was hypocrisy! Everything I had taught and been taught, what if it meant nothing?

Suddenly memory stretched back through my life … and I remembered everything … every infant terror, childhood humiliation, adolescent loneliness, Mother hanging in the blossoming apple tree … every thought I had ever had came rushing towards me at the same time like a pack of howling dogs. The research I had to do for studies I had to write for positions I had to strive for in countries I still had to visit

… How could I do *anything* when a thousand more urgent actions were screaming at me to be done?

I couldn't read a line in a book without the words fragmenting, like for Satsuki the sentences breaking down, and I had to make a huge effort to restore the syntax in my mind, and by that time any meaning the words had had were lost. The language might as well have been Finnish, or some foreign tongue I'd begun to study yesterday – and I could recognize that some words were similar to words in my own language, and so could vaguely construct a meaning, but whether this was the intended reading or not I couldn't know. In the words of Professor Heilbutt, I had no *Sprachgefühl* for my own language.

And because reading was impossible I tried to write, and though this was possible the words did exactly what they did when I only read; words written by my own hand lay as dead carcasses strewn across the page just as other people's words. Words, words, words, words, words, another word, one more word, oh here is a word, I found another one, you like words? Look, here's a big one! And so on. Even writing about and configuring the meaninglessness into words was meaningless. Was anything so absurd as trying to make sense of absurdity? So there was no point in doing anything or thinking anything or living anything. I could only do what I couldn't control – like breathing, pumping blood with my heart, willing myself with my entire being to hold together enough not to fragment and go mad. Defensive reflexes. But shouldn't a mindful, wilful, strong independent spirit like mine be able to stop its own blood flow?

*Its own blood flow.* That my body had become an "it" to me further proved that I was an it, that the world was an it, and that the plural of "it" was "nothing". But even "nothing" was something – it was a word that had meaning. The absence I felt was different. Language couldn't grasp it. Thought couldn't grasp it. But like the black dog of doubt still following me, it was there; my soul felt itself sliding in.

And then today I was myself again. I couldn't relate to yesterday's terror. When home, language, literature and research surrounded me it was hard to believe I had ever doubted them. That place in the mountains, the View of the Snow Country, had shrouded my view of things as they are; I'd returned infected with some contagious affliction rather than alpine clarity.

Had the doubt remained, I might even have checked myself into the clinic as a patient to investigate its cancer from eye-level. Instead, I finished these notes on my experience – the first instalment in my grand work of case studies – then posted an application letter to the renowned Esterházy clinic in Budapest, opened a manual written by the great Professor Heilbutt, and began to read.

❈ ❈ ❈ ❈ ❈

# RETURN OF THE PANCHEN LAMA

In a measure of goodwill before the 2008 Beijing Olympics, on his birthday China released the eleventh and true Panchen Lama, Gendhun Choekyi Nyima, political prisoner for the past thirteen years since the age of six. He was re-established in his rightful role as head abbot of the Tashilhunpo Monastery near Shigatse, and the impostor lama who had been installed in his place was removed. His Holiness the Dalai Lama and the Tibetan government in exile were also invited to return to the Potala winter palace in Lhasa.

We publicly welcomed both developments, but sixty years of abuses by China left us suspicious. A public relations move on the part of the Chinese, we surmised, one which would quickly become less generous once the Olympics were over. But if it temporarily raised China's standing internationally while permanently strengthening the Tibetan cause, then it was a positive development.

Politely we declined the offer to return home, where our every movement would be reported on, where every gesture would be misconstrued and used as propaganda against us, where every monastery harboured government spies in robes, and requested that the Pandita Chen-po Lama be allowed to travel to our base in Dharamsala, Himachal Pradesh. The Indian government, when it had its own grievances with China, once allowed us this Himalayan oasis and now was unsure what to do with us. But in a further public gesture of goodwill China complied, and the Panchen Lama came to meet the Dalai Lama for the first time in thirteen years.

The rest of the exiled cabinet and I were present at this historic meeting, the joining of the two greatest powers of Tibet. We hoped this would begin a new chapter of hope after sixty years of despair, that from this point forward we could begin a return to our nation and work to raise it to its former autonomy and glory.

His Holiness, though, at the meeting did something shocking. While polite to the boy, he used language one would use when addressing a member of a foreign religion, not as the long-lost and missing piece of the exiled government, the returned hope of his people. And he subjected the boy to the same tests – finding the belongings of his predecessor from the pile, questions on matters of scripture – he had passed fifteen years ago to be recognized as the reincarnated Panchen Lama.

When I showed him to his quarters, the boy did not seem offended to be so treated and then so quickly dismissed. His youthful face turned inward as he slipped into meditation with a clean expression, no visible antagonism towards anyone, even his former captors. He seemed too small for his robes; his smooth hands could have belonged to a girl, but the fingers of his right hand rotated around a small object, or an idea.

Later I requested an audience with His Holiness to seek an explanation for actions that contradicted his own teachings on hospitality, generosity and kindness.

"You believe the boy is a false lama?"

"He could easily pick out the belongings of his former incarnation," responded His Holiness. "He answered all the questions on scripture."

"Then you are forcing humility on him, so he can begin relearning his duties and his station?"

A sigh.

"You are establishing your authority over him?"

"He is not a true Tibetan."

"But without him Tibet is spiritually incomplete!"

"It is too late."

"Then what should we do with the boy?"

My master paused before answering. "He is tainted by his education. Though he thinks he is here to begin serving his people, he is here to undermine us." As if to dismiss me, he formed his meditation pose. When I rose to go, though, he whispered something, eyes closed. I asked him to repeat himself.

"It is my fault," he said. "I should have waited. I proclaimed him to the world as the lama reincarnate, showing the enemy exactly where to find the boy. We are lucky they didn't poison him."

"Let me teach him," I said. "Put me in charge of his reawakening."

"He might taint you too."

"Surely I'm beyond the influence of a teenager. Besides, what else can we do?"

"We can always wait for the next incarnation."

"That could take eighty years or more!"

"We can wait five hundred years if we must."

"There is another problem with that," I said.

"I know what you are thinking."

"If your present incarnation were to pass away ..."

"Then the Panchen Lama is in charge of choosing my successor. I am aware of that."

"He might bypass the rules of incarnation and choose a child more loyal to Beijing. For that reason alone, it is imperative I be in charge of his re-education."

"If you think it best."

For a time the boy, receiving no further audiences with His Holiness, worked on ingratiating himself with the others. I found him sincere and well intentioned, deferential and intelligent. The maturity of the wise, reverence of the sincere, curiosity of the young. He had intuitive understanding rather than a gift for words, and valued – like all spiritual people – moments of silence. I was happy to have him among us again. We walked silently in the gardens, and I could feel his strong and holy aura. We would look through the foliage and protective fences at the hundreds of daily pilgrims below who circled the compound to worship the knowledge that the two holiest figures in our culture lived within. He always used reverential language with me despite the fact only one man in the world existed above him. He was a keen observer and befriended the animals that roamed our little compound, as well as the Indian soldiers stationed just within the barbed wire.

I taught the boy our ways. I began from zero, and much of it he knew but there were gaping holes in his theory. He filled these gaps quickly; much I didn't have to explain to him, he picked it up intuitively. He was perhaps already closer to enlightenment than I will be in this incarnation.

When His Holiness heard how the boy was progressing and ingratiating himself, he seemed more disposed to the idea of giving him a position within the government. Our autonomy struggle going nowhere, our people still suffering, it made sense to use the boy as an envoy or figurehead. We began making exploratory overtures abroad, looking into cultural ambassadorships, representative powers in some new diplomatic capacity.

But one day the boy made a mistake that dashed my hopes for him.

"Why," he asked me, "do you hate the Chinese so much?"

His education was clear. How China had liberated his land from bickering sects, feuding lamas and oppressive landlords, unifying their great nations as they had been under the Mongol Empire – that China had done Tibet an unappreciated service of liberation. I saw he had been treated well by his kidnappers, but that his education had contained many side-truths and much subterfuge, that he was so far removed from the true experience of his people that His Holiness was right to ostracize him from our fragile administration. How could he guide a people he didn't understand into a future ruled from Beijing? Perhaps he had even been placed among us in order for China to get as much information as possible on the inner workings of a suspicious people.

"Forgive me for asking," he added.

I had never mentioned to the boy my feelings on the occupation or our occupiers – never mentioned that unlike His Holiness I advocated an unequivocal independence, through violent means if necessary. I had never mentioned to him – or even to His Holiness, who had fled the country when our Lhasa insurrection was clearly doomed – the great evils I'd witnessed under the occupation, the wanton destruction of temples and 6,000 monasteries, bonfires fuelled with holy scripture, the round-ups of monks and nuns, the torture of those who refused to renounce His Holiness, the arbitrary arrests and the killings and the starvation.

I'd never mentioned to the boy my fear for my life as I fled through the Himalayas with two fellow abbots, how we lost our way in the snowstorms around the Kanchenjunga pass, how only two of us finally made it into Sikkim in India, how we both lost toes or feet to the frost. Beijing has a million of our deaths on its conscience – or would if the government had a conscience. In sixty years of advocating loving kindness, I haven't been able to outgrow my hatred.

"I am Tibetan," insisted the boy. "Tibet is my country."

"I never said otherwise, Your Holiness."

"I submit my will to that of my people."

"Your people are happy to have you returned to us."

"Not all are happy."

The boy suffered in his political impotence. Even he, despite his divinity, felt a need to be needed. But he was here in the wrong guise, and we still needed the Panchen Lama who had been abducted thirteen years ago.

In a private audience with His Holiness we discussed what to do with the boy. Could we still make use of the lama within our government, or abroad or in Lhasa or Beijing to spread messages of peace and autonomy? Again we discussed more limited ambassadorships, having him rule the corridors of Potala, sending him on a tour of Western countries with myself at his side as adviser, and how to make him feel needed and at home.

We decided to raise our ideas with the grand committee and with the boy himself. There was no point keeping our feelings from him since he understood our thoughts quite clearly and was saddened by their negativity. In our hearts we knew whatever responsibilities we gave him would be hollow without our confidence in his judgement. We had the difficult task of making him feel useful while keeping to a minimum the damage he could do.

In the end the boy removed our quandaries for us. If he had considered it an option since the day he returned to us, or only now deemed it the only possible course, I am not sure. He must have brought the poison with him from China, perhaps even intended to be administered to His Holiness. There is a long tradition in our mythology of those obliged to administer poison at a given time, and if no one is present at the fatal instant the person must drink it himself. In this case, though, it seemed a carefully considered political decision.

When he died – solitary in his chamber, alone in the world – painfully in the poison's convulsions, he forever removed from us his gentle, beautiful and intelligent incarnation.

Currently His Holiness is seeking the twelfth manifestation of the Panchen Lama, so that we may raise him in our temple to be the voice and consciousness of his people, to one day raise our beleaguered nation again into lasting independence and peace.

❄ ❄ ❄ ❄ ❄

# THE UNDERWORLD

## I

They played hearts, passed a joint clockwise and diluted their Sangsom rum with bottled water. The two Europeans recapped a weekend journey into the wilderness pausing in Lisu or Lahu villages for meals and opium, while the boys concentrated on their cards and what conversation might be least destructive to later attempts at seducing the girls. Carlos, dealt a disastrous hand of aces and kings and the dreaded spade queen, decided to reverse his strategy and shoot the moon asking questions as he did hoping no one would notice. "What was it like with the Lahu elder? You do it standing up or sideways?"

Anne-Marie and Bridget paused, suggesting to David they worried Carlos had misinterpreted their story. Tall Anne-Marie possibly the nicer of the two, he thought, but a bit serious, too much Old Europe, goaded into intrepid treks by her friend with the accent that made him melt. If given a choice he'd take the less nice one, even with her largish hips and witch-like laugh.

"You mean the opium?" Bridget pronounced in her Irish lilt. She decided to hang on to her king of hearts in case that Mexican-American fraction-of-Jew oddball of ethnicity Carlos was up to something. "Lying down in a dark hut," she answered. "The only light came through the doorway or cracks in the wall like rays of gold. We inhaled through a long pipe the younger men lit for us." In one drawn-out motion she began the trick with a five of hearts, took a swig of Sangsom – quickly refilled by David from the big bottle – sat back and cackled. "They only wore pretty chequered sarong things round their waists. You know, their hard bodies, chests glistening with smoke and sweat."

Carlos followed too tentatively, stretching out an unsure hand and casually dropping the ace of hearts, which would win him the points. Now everyone was aware of what he was planning. "What was the feeling?" he asked at the faces looking at him with screwed up eyes.

"Of the opium? Just seemed to put me to sleep." As if the memory caught up with her, Anne-Marie yawned. You're not fooling anyone you know, she said with her eyes at him over the cards. There was something beyond his hesitations, though, that she liked. Perhaps in his trimmed goatee or the vaguely elegant way – high-neck Mon shirt, khaki trousers bought in South Africa – he dressed. Respectability was a rare feature in a traveller, especially an American.

It was Bridget from Galway who preferred questions she could elaborate on. Leaving Europe for the first time should have been the best part, she'd thought, but every single day here was another adventure, a new wonder. "A five-hour spell of colour-rich vision," she spoke with glinting eyes, "white shaking at the edges, nauseous stomach, alternate lightness and heaviness, the irrepressible urge to laugh at the painful things memory brings forth. Kind of like a dream you have control of," she added, "with the world in slow motion. More things that aren't quite there, peripheral."

She smiled. Our feet never touched ground, she remembered to herself. We followed the trails, gazing at maps, covering just two miles an hour. Stopping for the pretty natural things you always pass without noticing. What depth and texture a simple teak tree, reduced to any square inch, could have! If we met a roving hill tribesman in the woods we'd break into a grin and he'd break into a grin and we'd keep on going.

She took a drink. The asterisk of a mosquito settled between her knuckles. She played the king of hearts she had saved, sacrificing a few points – it was, after all, the suicide king, sword thrust into his own temple – for the sake of foiling Carlos, who had to eat his own queen of spades and, when the points were tallied, lost the game.

"Me again?" Bridget happy in her victory shook her hand to clear it of mosquitoes as David opened another bottle and Anne-Marie lit another joint.

To fill the time of shuffling the deck conversation turned to the country's far north and its poppy-rich Golden Triangle, which three of the four of them had already visited. "In Chiang Rai this girl came to my door one night," David said, his Queensland nasality thickening with every glass of rum, "and in decent English asked if I wanted her to spend the night."

"And what did you say?" Anne-Marie raised her eyebrows. Her right hand tried to fit behind her ear the bangs she had decided to grow out. Brown strands, though, still fell over her eyes. Her language had a trace of East London though she had been raised in Holland. Working in England for several years she had met Bridget through a common boyfriend. He had been dropped, they had kept in touch and now were six months together on a round-the-world ticket.

David had expected them to take his refusal in Chiang Rai for granted and hesitated on the verge of an untruth. In the end he shrugged. "I told her to come back in an hour."

The girls studied rum glass or fingernails with what he thought was interest. Only Carlos dazed of disapproval. It pleased David that a confession that might have been disastrous for his triple prospects for another game and another bottle and sex with Bridget seemed not to have hurt his strategy at all.

"How much was she asking?" Carlos asked. Slowly he took a drink, wincing through the aftertaste, and stared away into the dark.

David studied the American for a moment. The night before he had deemed him too educated, or travelled. Or pedantic when the world was discussed. Most annoying was that if you complained about something specific here, he would say *Well you should go to Vietnam, where* ... He had been anywhere you discussed and knew all the facts. He could probably not only name every capital city in the world but every currency, or national language, or major export. Competitive enough with them to be irritating. Tonight he had seemed uneasy, shy maybe, boring. Nice guy, David thought, but too slow for these girls.

"She wanted seven hundred baht," he said, "but I talked her down to five."

The women's only disapproval was that he would haggle over a companion for the night over a difference of three quid.

"She wasn't some fourteen-year-old village girl forced to by debt-ridden parents?" Carlos had heard of such things, and suspected David might have no moral spine.

"She was no virgin," David answered wryly in Gold Coast under-statement.

Anne-Marie said, "And were you proud of yourself? Feel more of a man?"

"Felt sleazy paying for pussy when it's not exactly hard to come by!"

It had been the Sangsom talking. The vulgarity had hurt his chances, David noted, both girls wrinkling up their mouths in distaste. He emphasized drunkenness by further thickening his natural drawl. "Felt kind of hollow, doing one of those odious acts you'd thought only guys who flaunted themselves in locker rooms would ever do then talk about like some badge of manhood." He looked from one face to the other to assess the damage done and the success of his attempt to patch it up again. "Not to be repeated by me, no, were his famous last words ... Another game?"

Bridget's shrug expressed a measure of Celtic endorsement. "If I was a man I might have done it."

"Maybe me too," Anne-Marie admitted quietly, with a glance at Carlos.

Carlos interposed his opinion finally as David dealt. The conversation had extended beyond the bounds of a morality he had for months been trying to define and come to terms with. He spoke of perpetuating systems, robbing dignity, killing social standing, encouraging others to do the same – demean themselves for a few easy baht and catch diseases which were spread in turn.

"Hey all precautions were taken," David defended himself in this regard. "And you have the oldest profession in every culture in the world."

"When a foreigner fetishizes local girls ..." Carlos began a little helplessly, moving his arms to express what he couldn't. "It's orientalism ... denigration of the other. Setting a bad example ..."

It had never been David's intention to set examples. He wanted to do the things he did because he did them. Being himself had always made up for what he couldn't be; people appreciated the fact they could reach him.

"In every country a woman's a woman," he said.

The girls were content to follow the discussion and play their hands. Cigarette smoke mingled with mosquito coil threads in the warm darkness. Carlos drained his glass and picked up the cards. He knew he would lose again. A lifetime of tolerance at stake, he probed the women with a glare until Bridget admitted, "Hate to say it, but I've known enough of guys to know they're incorrigible."

"The fact something happens doesn't mean it's *right*," Carlos tried again, hands reaching at the air as much in opposition to the new cards he was dealt as a need to follow the argument. He looked at Bridget and Anne-Marie still organizing their cards and felt nostalgia for some past age of innocence he couldn't pinpoint.

David was meanwhile suggesting that in films, in fashion magazines, in pulp romances, the romanticized prostitute story – the whore turned princess – appealed even more to women than men.

"Here's where I draw the line," Anne-Marie said, taking a sharper drag. Straightening her back she smiled slightly to show her objection was more an act of conditioned negation than deep-felt. "That is another matter entirely. What you unmarried boys do is your business but don't think we *approve*!"

Kreangsak, son of the owners of the Mountain Wilderness Guest Home, back home for summer holidays from university in the capital, climbed the steps to the veranda. An apologetic index finger to his smile indicated that alcohol had inflated their voices and some of the guests had long since gone to bed.

Carlos, drained from clinging to principles that failed to impress even himself, welcomed the diversion. Through all his travels, any distinctions he learned to make, any inspired moment of moral clarity, inevitably clouded. "What've you done today, Kreang?"

"Five day trekking group. Rain put off one day. Try again in the morning." Kreangsak paused, wondering if it would be bad form to make a sales pitch to a group he had got staggering drunk with only the night before. He smiled. "You want join?"

"We just did our own trek," Bridget lilted proudly. "Walked and walked into woods and mountains and came back safe and sound."

David loved the way she said sound. Or mountains. Or anything. He refilled the empty glasses with ice and rum and, picking out one of his strands of red hair, left out the water. "You want some?"

Kreangsak, retracting to the kitchen for a glass, came back prepared with another pitch. "There other things not trekking," he said. "You know?" And he spoke of Pai River rafting, elephant camps, the Doi Inthanon National Park for black bears or waterfalls. Macaques, monkeys, gibbons, deer. Mountain villages for handicrafts. Spelunking organized with lights and ropes and local guides. One opened into a cavern full of bats during the day and swallows at night – at dusk and dawn you saw them swapping places, one current above the other. Enough flapping bodies to block out the sky. And there was a long narrow cave called *Tham Narok*, or Hell Hole. You had to squirm through it and it was so deep no one had ever found the end. Somewhere in the middle depths, according to legend, was a legendary carved Wall of Faces no Westerner had ever seen.

"I like the sound of that," David conceded as he crunched through an ice cube. Hell Hole. Wall of Faces. It sounded spiritual. Or perhaps the antithesis of spiritual. Dark.

"My cousin take you tomorrow, six hundred baht for group." Kreangsak, tasting his drink, gave a slight shudder and added water. His student life had taught him to drink but his friends in the capital, to highlight a perceived social standing, drank only imported Scotch.

Bridget excused herself and Anne-Marie from potential outings, as they were leaving for Mae Hong Son in the morning.

"Too bad," David said to her, grazing her bare knee lightly with his fingertips. "It might have been romantic."

For a while Kreangsak sat thinking and smoking cigarettes. He watched the four play their hands, declining to join them. Hearts couldn't be played with five. His body when he sat always harboured a restlessness that made at least one leg twitch. The eye-contact shuffling between David and Bridget like a shuttlecock – batted straight, then sinking suddenly – annoyed him, which made his leg twitch even more persistently. He could never behave like that, nor would any good Thai girl.

With a tone of dawning inspiration he suddenly said, "Everyone sleep but I drive you there now! Only look. In a cave no matter what time." Seeing the sceptical faces of Carlos and the girls, he felt guilty for having tried to sell his new friends a trekking package. Knowing his father would object, he added, "No money. Just show you and come back. Maybe we don't find it in dark. But the moon almost full. If rain cloud don't come back."

David looked at the others with an unspoken query. No expression fashioned any objection he could recognize, so he placed his cards face down on the table just in case he would have to pick them up again. "Let's go!"

The four warmed to the idea as Kreangsak began remembering obstacles. Even if he found the entrance they'd get filthy dirty like they couldn't imagine. They should wear only shoes with the best traction and the most useless tight-fitting clothing – with pockets for spare batteries and light bulbs. In case the torches went dim. If anyone was claustrophobic, not in good physical shape or not willing to absolve him of responsibility in case of torn clothes or lost contact lens or broken leg then they probably shouldn't go.

He looked from one face to the other but they didn't seem put off. The girls hurried to their bungalow and the boys to both of theirs to change or snack on the bananas haggled for at market only a few hours before. Kreangsak, left leg twitching, sat alone with nothing to do but light another cigarette and pour himself another glass of Sangsom from the abandoned bottle.

# II

He tried to change course. His father's red Isuzu short-bed bounced over potted dirt trails to the wide-mouthed cave full of swallows now and bats by day. But the girls in the cab, preferring narrow muddy tunnels to caverns glazed with guano, redirected him. So as David and Carlos continued a heated discussion in the back – they could hear various notes and see the mouthing of it when they turned around – Kreangsak drove eight kilometres over clay roads slippery and puddled by recent rains in the direction of the passage he called Hell Hole.

"The entrance we walk from here." He parked the truck by the painted stump marker he recognized. Standing under bright pulsing stars and moonshine together they felt giddily adventurous. "Too much rain. Cave maybe slippery."

Even Carlos waved his hand at the irrelevance, impatient to enter small damp dark worlds with names suggestive of damnation. Since antiquity, the Underworld had commanded a fascination. Now, after the argument in the back of the truck – David claiming the girls were up for it and Carlos' stolidity was putting them off – he felt vaguely classical. He wanted to woo women or battle the hounds of Hades.

Kreangsak distributed electric torches and more batteries and spare bulbs than the four had pockets for. The miner-style head lamps, he apologized, and other equipment were in the hands of the local guide for the night.

As they trekked into the jungle Anne-Marie told more of her opium experience. "Remember, Bridget …?" And spoke of the white mushrooms growing, white flowers moving, shimmering in the trees, sleepily laughing, the ground breathing beneath their feet …

The girls laughed at the memory of reality turned abstract and the mood was contagious. Kreangsak, coil of rope hanging from his shoulder, led them through the trees with long strides. Carlos moved into step just behind Anne-Marie. David patted his stomach and remembered his Chiang Rai prostitute with increasing fondness. They walked through the undergrowth over damp twigs and fallen bamboo, scratched at by hardwoods, casting their lights in short arcs trying not to venture from the single track trail and hoping to avoid puddles.

The terrain began shifting under their lights. Going uphill, the soft decaying matter underfoot turned to stone and root. No longer laughing they concentrated on the sobering twists of switchback, stirring the air around their heads with fingers trying to disperse insects. When they broke a sweat they remembered that even in the highlands past the hot season this was still the tropics.

Kreangsak surprised himself by finding it. He stood over a clump of rocks victoriously while the others paused, waiting for him to go on or give the speech he seemed on the verge of.

"This is it."

"What, here?" Bridget looked around, then down at the edges of the two-foot-wide hole her light found and failed to penetrate. "It's nothing but a bloody rabbit hole!"

Kreangsak smiled at the general sinking of resolve and purpose. But rather than stand there shifting while insects filled on their blood, first Carlos then the women then David followed his example, squirming feet first through films of cobwebs and scuttling sounds. From below Kreangsak guided their shoes to footholds, holding their calves as they fumbled on the slippery surfaces. Until they stood on solid ground within Hell Hole, the night sky framed circular above. Torchlight intersecting the small chamber, the four inspected where they were to find on all sides only glistening rock and clay and root.

Bridget casting the light over herself pouted, "I'm filthy already!" David thought she looked beautiful, streaks of red clay on her freckled arms, damp T-shirt bearing Hard Rock Café Saigon that in the cave light matched the depth of her thin brown hair. Against the harsh craggy background she looked exquisitely soft.

"You see?" said Kreangsak. The four had to follow the shaft of his light. He was pointing at a small plump, Chinese-style Buddha – not the local androgynous kind – bronze, perched near the ceiling on a miniature outcrop.

"It's beautiful," Anne-Marie chimed.

"It's Buddha-ful," David corrected.

Kreangsak lit a half-melted candle fitted below the Buddha, and to Carlos the way it had previously melted looked obscenely phallic. "That's not a candle," he said, trying to top David, "but a scandal." He could see through the flickering shades deep shadows in the faces of his companions.

Bridget aimed the light into holes looking for passages but her guide, worried he was forgetting something, had to illuminate the one under her feet. "Careful. I don't know it so slippery. Me first."

This time his slim, dark athletic body disappeared head-first, both arms pointed into the emptiness in front of him as if diving in slow motion into a pool of solid rock. "It squeeze," he had explained to them, lips fumbling around the word squeeze. "Breathe out and push through like snake, use finger, toe, move muscle. Breathe in at wrong time and you stuck. Got it?"

When the girls emerged first he guided their bodies with his palms reminding them to exhale then push. Bridget's hips wedged into the rock, the front and tail of her wagging helplessly. When she inhaled the walls touched every part of her body, the entire tunnel fit her like a cast. From ahead she was pulled and from behind pushed, one set of hands pressing into the softness of her upper thighs until with a slight ripping sound as a piece of her jeans lingered behind she was through and they continued.

They never stood again. When the ceiling rose it granted enough space to sit up in the slipperiness, water falling through the pores in the rock and dirt onto their heads, but never to stand. Most of the passage they could only cover the muddy ground in single file following the beacon of the light ahead. Descending the night in purple through stale air.

After an hour of tunnels rubbing clay over them, Kreangsak stopped in a cavern large enough for them to assemble. Seated cross-legged, they enjoyed the pressure of bodies on either side. They had stopped and so the direction they were going in had stopped.

"Glad I'm not claustrophobic," whispered Bridget.

"Maybe we can't go more," Kreangsak said. More worrying to him than the wetness that had rendered the tunnels almost unnavigable was what he had forgotten: the requisite prayer for protection at the entrance Buddha.

The women were relieved, Bridget thinking there were three guys anyway which upset the balance. Kreangsak's lithe ease with the terrain was disturbingly sensual.

Carlos and David pondered the ill fortune of an adventure cut short just as it started bordering on intrepid. This was the start of what might pass for a travel tale once they returned home. In David's eyes in a momentary flashlight glare Carlos thought he caught hint of a confirmation so subtle as to make it unmistakable.

He said, "Can Dave and I keep going a ways on our own?"

Even David looked dubious. Carlos wondered if he had misread him. Anne-Marie's voice from the other side of the chamber carried more reproach than he felt was necessary. "Well Bridget and I can't wait at the entrance for you forever. We have to leave in the morning and still haven't packed!"

"We can meet back at the guesthouse in the morning. Only a short walk to the road when we're done. We can catch a *songthaew*, or if they're not running yet just start walking."

To Kreangsak the idea didn't sound entirely faulty – his task would be returning two drunk pretty European girls safely home. But he caught a sense of the irresponsibility of it and what his father would shout if anything went wrong.

"Tunnel split and go maybe forever and now more dangerous with the wet!"

But the possibility had taken root in David and he didn't want to leave Carlos alone in his inspiration. The girls would think he was afraid. "We'd be safe," he reassured, "making sure we go back the way we came." Still sensing objection he added, "We only want to go a little way. Don't worry, we absolve you of responsibility if Carlos breaks his skull and I have to haul him out."

For Kreangsak this was enough but Anne-Marie said, "Go home, rest up, and in the morning hire a guide if you still want."

"In the morning we'll start at the rum again," Carlos admitted. To him, Anne-Marie's seated shadow now seemed too tall to be attractive, and her voice too rough, fraying him like the jagged tunnels. "It's now or never."

In the lamp-lit dark Bridget with her voice lifted hands in resignation. Mimicking Anne-Marie's declaration from earlier, she said, "What you eejits do is your business, just don't think we approve!"

Carlos and David not even looking at her prodded at the twinkling wet walls with their eyes and lights for a way forward. Kreangsak, sensing his authority slipping, checked their torches again to make sure both worked and gave them more spare batteries and bulbs in case they stayed longer than planned.

So with the women squirming their way back out, Bridget at the head not even able to turn back to say goodbye, Kreangsak gave a last plea not to make trouble for him by getting lost. David and Carlos waved hands and shrugged shoulders, focusing away from him into the inviting folds of the rock.

"They say you go deep there is the Wall of Faces," Kreangsak added. "Carved by a tribe thousand year ago. Has strange power. You ask and wall will answer, maybe before you ask. Not many have seen."

In better spirits Kreangsak left them the blue coil of nylon rope and guided the womens' bodies with his hands where they needed pressure. Anne-Marie's calves and feet under his gently placed palms were more or less unresponsive, Bridget's warm thighs gave the faintest hint of reacting pressure. At one point when she got stuck he thought it might have been deliberate, so he could place both palms gently on the fleshy seat of her torn jeans and give slow upward forward thrusts as she wriggled.

When they reached the mouth again bowing thanks to the bronze perched Buddha, rain fell through the small hole in the ceiling. The wax obscenity had burned itself out. Kreangsak pulled at the slippery edges of the hole, sliding at the wall with his feet, and hauled himself through. He grabbed Anne-Marie's then Bridget's hands and feeling strong pulled them clear. Thickening rain forced them to hurry back to the truck over uneven trail, but now it was downhill and they were laughing as they ran.

# III

Carlos and David were careful, marking in the mud as they went and where there was no mud scratching arrows in the rock with one of the many spare batteries. The tunnel didn't fork often and when it did one direction invariably funnelled into a dead end. They felt confident easing through holes tight and caked with moist pink clay.

"Sorry to see the girls go," David said, feeling completely sober now. The long passage of grunts and groans had gone wordless long enough. "Kreang the opportunist bastard might take advantage of the mood we worked so hard to put them in."

"I think they were lesbians," Carlos consoled from behind – a grasp at humour that missed.

The tunnel angled more steeply. For added traction they clung to the sides with battered fingernails. Tying the rope around a finger of rock, they held on as they slid down the ribbed throat of Hell Hole. Wet walls made a sucking sound as they went. When their toes found solidity beneath them they left the rope as marker. "Won't need it again," David said. "If we do we'll just head back."

On hands and knees they crawled, bruises spreading over joints from pulling and pushing their bodies through spaces that didn't want them. Rocky friction had frayed the seams of David's jeans and shredded Carlos's cotton trousers. Legs bled lengthwise. Neither complained, the twists of the tunnel demanding too much concentration. Carlos wondered if the Wall of Faces really existed. David with mental fingertips retraced the brown silken curves of his Chiang Rai girl's body, dimly aware that the longer they now descended the longer would be the return journey. But they had all night. Hell, he had the rest of the year, and didn't feel tired even after the bottles of Sangsom and hours of predatory forethought. Recalling the conversation over their game of hearts he felt vaguely satisfied at having loved a girl for a night and in the morning left her behind without pretence or subterfuge. He remembered her clearly now. Tian, she had said her name was as she dressed slowly, exposing her body and her smile to him one last time. Thin hard brown thighs, skin smooth as a baby's – it caught hold in his throat for an instant. If not for the physical effort of hoisting himself over stretches of rock falling away into nothingness he might have felt the warming in his abdomen turn to arousal.

Hearing something in its flight drop against distant walls he felt at his pockets now shorn through. His spare batteries were gone. He stood almost upright for the first time in Hell Hole. Reading a ledge with his toes, he leaned against the rock face trying to flatten his palms against the rock.

Carlos inching along behind tried to remember mythology he had been taught not so long ago in high school. It had fascinated him for a semester, then quickly been forgotten. Journeys by heroes into Hades, which seemed to resemble the current underworld. Orpheus, to retrieve Euridice, had journeyed down. And Odysseus, for directions to Ithaca, hoping to find the prophet Teiresias. Psyche seeking beauty in a box. And Aeneas, and all the others who had willingly descended and sometimes risen again.

If he and Dave were already in the Underworld, he realized, it meant not that death was a danger but that they were already stepping through a sphere of the no longer living. Beyond Erebus, now into Tartarus, beneath the secret passages of the earth. He was Theseus, Dave was Pirithoüs, trying to abduct Persephone. They would instead be led to the Chair of Forgetfulness where, minds blank, they would sit for the rest of eternity. Unless Hercules, while on the last of his twelve labours, rescued them. But that was another matter.

Dave ahead suddenly stepped into nothingness. He vanished, grunts heard banging down. For Carlos the dream effect dispersed. Focusing, squinting, he shone the light down a narrow hole that twisted but revealed no sign of his friend of two days.

"Where the hell are you?"

The wheezing reply like a faint echo curled up to him out of darkness: "No worries ... I'm alive."

"Well get up here again!"

Holding himself only with hands and feet clawing at the sides, David thought he'd never heard anything so annoying. Below him nothing he could see. Torchlight angled down but in the light was only more dark. He clung harder and when his breathing slowed enough, inch by inch crawled up again. Until Carlos saw his light, could reach down and when he had squirmed close enough give him a hand.

Back on the ledge, David gave a deep sigh and a shudder. "Mind the gap."

"Don't disappear like that!"

The other edge of the cavern offered a choice of three tunnels, with little distinguishing one from another. This time Carlos slithered in first. David paused to urinate into the pit they had crossed, distressed not to hear an echo. Only the sound of Carlos grunting in the tunnel ahead and the little drip and sucking sounds the walls seemed to shimmer with.

Exhaling, writhing through tight spots as Kreangsak had taught, they slid farther into long craggy tubes like the bowels of a petrified giant. David worried they had ventured far enough, but the terror of his fall had given him a second wind and Carlos betrayed no second thoughts.

Carlos at the front grew into his authority, resolving to find the Wall of Faces if it existed. Even the realization they had been forgetting to leave markers didn't dampen his mood, nor that his torch had gradually but surely grown dimmer. He tried to remember some of the people he had met while travelling through the continent during the past few months. All those who had done their part to ease him out of the bruising loneliness he had confided to none of them.

Through Sumatra he had paired with Pavel, a lanky Czech on an ambiguous business trip. On Koh Phi Phi he had fallen in love with a Scandinavian girl with sun-bleached hair, a heroin addiction and a perfectly shaped nose. She had made him the envy of solo travelling men battling romantic vertigo. There was that Dutchman in Kathmandu who had seen his daughter stillborn in Rotterdam and the next day decided to go find some mountains to climb. The Welsh girl whose parents had died in a car crash and who on the inheritance had tried to bury the past by crossing China by train. The American journalist he had had a beer with in Karachi who three weeks later, as he read in the *Herald Tribune*, was killed in Kabul not by Taliban incursion but a wayward supply truck.

Then Carlos arrived. When the tunnel ended, in the haze of his torch with sudden intake of breath he caught sight of the Wall of Faces. His entire life was etched into it. Everyone he had ever known. The history of civilization. He paused, blinking, and knew he had just lost his soul.

A chasm separated him from the faces, but a ledge offered a rock on which to sit and dangle legs over nothingness. His very own Chair of Forgetfulness, perched opposite the unforgettable.

David was slow to emerge, Carlos wondering if he had lost him. But Dave's head appeared, also gripped and dazed by this visit to magnificence, groping with his eyes at the wall in silence then complaining about his nearly dead torch and asking Carlos for spare batteries.

The new light uncovered heads of humans and animals in bas-relief, such as Carlos had seen at Angkor Wat while the temple girls had played with his hair. Immediately the hemisphere he called home vanished. He followed lines of bulls marching towards victory over a brutal god-king. He saw the locals of the countries he had passed through, ashamed for not having remembered them first. Like the Chinese Malaysians who had taught him proper left and right uppercuts and introduced him to a different underworld of gambling and moonshine. The entire village in Kerala which had descended into trance, penitents piercing cheeks and tongues, steel rods through their heads only for the wounds to go right through the body and come out in the morning without a scratch. Everywhere the smiles or glares of contempt. The mist surrounding girls working highland Philippine terraces, who had paused to smile just long enough for him to melt again into vertigo.

David also found those he knew and loved in the ambiguous designs and wondered how it had come to be, who had dared to carve on unreachable walls all the myths and memories crowding his, David's, own fantasies. The figures extended in all directions as far as the light, anything he had ever imagined seemed to exist here, rich in perfectly preserved detail. Although he knew none of it was real, it was. In fact it was reassuring. Tian whispering I want you. His father mouthing Come home son we miss you. Even Bridget and Anne-Marie were there grinning If you hadn't wanted so hard to be he-boys floundering in tunnels you could have got laid tonight. Which made him laugh. Then the number of characters in a Russian novel he was reading with their patronymics, diminutives, maiden names he had dutifully kept track of on pages of notes before giving up – now all came alive and continued dialogues that chapter breaks had brought to a close, and the dead were resurrected so their love affairs could continue in their turbulence.

Carlos's light flickered just enough to make both retreat to practical problems.

"Think we have enough light left to make it back out?" David asked.

"Maybe if we only use one flashlight at a time. We've been in here a few hours too many."

Carlos as he said this realized it hardly mattered now. They were spirits wandering the underworld, already accepted by the landscape. Vertical campaigns were no longer possible. In the wall he saw Cerberus, dragon tail whipping up the dust and triple head panting triple forked tongues, and the three judges who would condemn them to eternal torture or the Elysian Fields. Chasms below and around were the rivers they had crossed – the Phlegethon, Styx and Lethe. On their thrones immortal in the rock sat Hades and Persephone themselves, greeting his soul into the afterworld.

But with a shrug he followed David. The air seemed thinner now as he wondered how much oxygen existed way down here. Back in the tunnel they crawled the way they had come, back behind the line where knowledge would again be useful, where they could depend on habit for substance in a life of drifting through.

In the chamber where David had fallen they found many passages all looking like the one that had brought them here. Sleepily they argued over it and Carlos let David win, extinguishing his own light as he followed Dave's. The tunnel wasn't one they recognized, and at the end of it rose a sheer wall. Sliding backwards they returned to the cavern. Carlos picked a new direction, after a tortuous hour it ending much the same, their heads poked over nothingness.

They looked everywhere, one by one over the hours tried every passage leading out of the one cavern they were positive they recognized. In the end, with dimmer light and thinner patience, they only reached the Wall of Faces once again. They sat silently pondering options.

"What time do you think it is?"

"Daytime. I don't know, maybe nearing noon."

High noon. On his travels it had always been his meeting time. Meet you at noon at the Acropolis. At noon at the National Museum. At noon at the Winter Palace. Now Carlos could add one more appointment: at noon we'll have lost our way in an underground cave to sit and watch the lights go dim and feel the oxygen contract.

"Think they'll realize we're not back yet?"

"Maybe, but there's not much they can do about it."

David pondered the fact of this. Even a hastily assembled search party might never find them, hours deep in an underground labyrinth made almost impassable by the seasonal rains. Or the girls would leave without realizing they were missing. Kreangsak to defend himself from his father would claim ignorance. And no one would notice their absence. Well, until whoever came to clean the bungalows found their rucksacks, but what could they do then?

He watched the wall go blank and remembered a report of some woman in Italy spending six months underground sealed away for the sake of science, watching her body slow to forty-hour days in a permanence of dark and silence. And here he was, doing the same but not by choice. It had been a choice yesterday or this morning but no longer.

Their one functioning torch had little power left. They turned it off to sit in darkness so complete it took their breath away.

Carlos thought David not a bad person to sit here with. A new friend with whom to vacillate towards that other darkness. The biggest regret was how their one-way journey into earth would appear to those who eventually came to think about and look for them and found nothing. No, his biggest regret was not kissing Anne-Marie.

"Remember the hearts game we never finished?" David asked in the dark.

Carlos nodded and then, realizing his invisibility, said yes.

"Do you remember what your hand was?"

And so with the girls as ghost hands they sat pondering strategy, speaking out loud the cards they played in order to endure and to forget, through a dream as infallible as opium's, their fall from responsibility, their failure, the nullity hanging over them like disgrace. And at the end of each round they tallied the total.

✳ ✳ ✳ ✳ ✳

# THE HOUSEKEEPER

When Arai Tomohiro came home from his usual walk in the park, a strange woman stood in his kitchen. Through the window from outside he saw her transplanting some herb – basil, mint? – from a small pot into a bigger pot. She looked about his age, with greying hair, bent over the counter. For a moment he wondered if it was the right apartment, if he in fact lived here, and had to check the name above the letter slot. To his relief, it spelled Arai, with the right two characters. After the relief, though, came worry. He had to do something about this. In his work there had been a protocol for every circumstance, and bosses to take over complications that rose above his training. In a situation like this, Tanihara would have told him what to do. What would his boss tell him now? Call the police – is that what he'd say? But perhaps it was just a simple mistake by the woman – maybe her mind was feeble in old age. In that case she didn't need to be harassed and arrested and shocked that much closer to death. Tanihara would have told him to gently escort the woman out and find out where she lived and call her a taxi. This, in the end, was what Arai decided to do.

He walked in and loudly – he didn't want to sneak up behind an old woman and scare her to death – said, "I'm home."

"Welcome back," she replied, without pausing from the ministrations of the plant.

Strange woman! He hovered in the kitchen doorway.

"Are you hungry?" she asked.

"I ate a crepe in the park."

"You shouldn't have spoiled your appetite!"

Herb finally packed in soil in an earthenware pot, she turned to face him. "What's wrong with you? You look like you've seen a ghost."

He gave a weak smile. "Who are you?"

She laughed. "What a question! I haven't changed in ages. For want of a name you might actually remember, I suppose you could call me your housekeeper!"

He was relieved, and his face and shoulders relaxed. He must have hired her and then forgotten about it. Recently, such things were becoming possible. He'd become forgetful. Perhaps a neighbour had introduced or recommended her, or he had seen an ad and hired her, or maybe his old company had provided her, and it had all been so effortless he'd forgotten the matter. And when he looked at her closely now, she did seem a bit familiar.

When he had retired at the usual age there had been the worry he might not be able to manage on his own. For decades he'd eaten lunch in the company cafeteria and dinner at hostess and snack bars. On a Sunday he would have bought a convenience store bento or heated up some water for cup noodles. With his pension he couldn't afford the bars; they would have to become weekly excursions rather than daily ones. He ventured to supermarkets for food instead of just beer and snacks. And since he had no idea how to cook, he had mused over the idea of employing someone to come once in a while and do a bit of cooking and cleaning. Of course, it would be expensive, impractical maybe, but it had been a hopeful thought.

She served a meal of *nimono*, salad and grilled mackerel and poured him a glass of Sapporo black label. She seemed to be able to intuit what he wanted before he asked for it. He'd never imagined a housekeeper could be so great to have around. But what had he agreed to pay her? As long as it was affordable, she was worth it. Maybe, he thought optimistically, his company had agreed to pay part of her wages as part of his retirement package.

"Shiozawa's wife Mikiko," she was saying, "told me today – don't tell anyone! – that since Shiozawa retired she can't stand the sight of him. He doesn't know how to do anything! He can't even withdraw money from the teller machine without her help, and she's fed up with his useless puttering around the house. He's worse than a baby, she says, without being cute at all!"

Some consternation must have clouded Arai's face, because she added lightly, "You may be useless too, but I still enjoy looking after you!"

She cleaned up the kitchen as he watched television, and after washing the dishes she joined him. Together they watched a Beat Takeshi variety show. He was surprised when later she took out and unfolded two futons on the tatami floor, with only about one mat distance separating them.

"You're staying?" he asked hesitantly.

Again she laughed. "Where would I go?" She wrinkled up her lips and after a pause added in a worried tone, "I shouldn't have told you about the Shiozawas."

He didn't really mind. The apartment was large enough for two, perhaps even too large for one, and he supposed she could stay if she had nowhere to go, or if she was so lonely on her own, or if that was what they'd arranged when he'd hired her. Besides, she would be there to prepare breakfast. Maybe she wouldn't mind doing the laundry.

The postman came in the morning, and as was customary he knocked on the door rather than stuff envelopes through impersonal mail slots.

Arai greeted him – though he couldn't, straining his memory, recall the man's name – and took the mail, a phone bill from NTT and a letter from his old company.

"How's the gateball game coming?"

"Oh, you know. At my age you can't really improve any more."

The housekeeper was humming the *Winter Sonata* theme tune in the kitchen, and the postman heard it.

"Not my taste, those Korean soap operas."

"Just for old women, I suppose."

"Does your wife play gateball too?"

"Oh, she's not …" Arai stopped himself in time. In the *genkan* were several pairs of shoes and some of them were women's shoes. Perhaps the pair of futons was still laid out and visible from the doorway. It would be obvious the woman had stayed the night. What would the postman think? It would be quite scandalous – and at his age! – to have rumours spread of how Arai had seduced his housekeeper.

"… very good," he finished.

The postman chuckled and continued on his rounds. Arai in the doorway opened the letters. His company had sent a note to those recently retired, thanking them for their years of service to the company and wishing them luck in their hobbies, travels, volunteer work or whatever else they were planning with their hard-earned free time. Though it was a simple form letter, Arai thought it a nice gesture. The newspapers were full of stories of men feeling lost and useless in retirement, of families breaking apart under the new stress of *time*, and his company wanted to make sure its former employees had a healthy and fulfilling second life. His letter was even signed by Tanihara, his former section manager. He had a lot of questions for Tanihara-san now, but he supposed he was on his own.

The phone bill had an itemized list of long-distance calls, and he glanced over them. Something was wrong. There were three calls to

Hiroshima and one as far away as Fukuoka. There was even a short but expensive call to America! He didn't know anyone in those places. Should he complain to NTT? Or … was it the housekeeper? This was going too far! She kept insinuating herself into his life and it was important he kept the boundaries of his independence clear.

Not without a touch of anger he approached the woman as she was feeding his clothes into the washing machine. "Did you call Hiroshima three times?" His voice trembled.

She looked surprised. "Mother's not feeling well, you know. She's getting headaches, and I'm a little worried about her living in that horrible institution."

"Well I'm not sure I can afford all these long-distance calls on my pension!"

She laughed. "You really are quite nit-picking and miserly in retirement!"

He felt guilty. It was only a few calls to her sick ancient mother, costing what – the same as a couple bottles of beer? It wasn't harming anyone. And considering all the things the woman was willing to do for him around the house she had the right to make a phone call now and then when he went out for his walks or his weekly game of gateball.

"Sorry," he muttered quietly, but the woman only laughed.


When he returned from his walk, the housekeeper looked up from a travel magazine.

"I have an idea," she said. "There are some good bus tours of Shinshu, to places like Kamikochi in the Alps, or the sulphur hot springs at Nozawa Onsen – why don't we go? It's not like you don't have the time."

"Can we afford it?"

"Stop being such a miser! It would only cost about twenty thousand yen a day for both of us, including the bus and guide and the inn."

"That's quite reasonable," he had to admit.

The strangest thing, it seemed to him as they left for the mountains, was not how easily and quickly the woman had worked her way into his life but how naturally other couples and fellow bus travellers accepted them. All assumed they had been married for decades, and it was a greater nuisance to set people straight than to just play along. And what was the difference? They were enjoying their little pilgrimage to the Alps. Did age have to stop a man from going on excursions with a woman whose company he enjoyed? Had they been married for forty years they might have enjoyed the trip in the same way, as a breach from the everyday.

And if he invented a collective past for them, told people of their arranged marriage in '66, their honeymoon in Hawaii, their daughter married to a Fukuoka publisher and their son apprenticed in California – who wouldn't believe it? And what would it matter if it wasn't true?

❈ ❈ ❈ ❈ ❈

# THE DEPARTURE

## I

A thirteen-year-old arrived at Manila International Airport escorted by her relatives and three boys none of them knew. The family carried among Nena's bags a vertiginous sadness, and Balthazar, her uncle, saw dark omen in the travelled faces of the airport crowd and in the oddly decorated walls and in the checked patterns of the floor tiles. He couldn't clear from his mind his grandfather's warning that the healer should never cross the waters. The fact that Grandfather had been the last healer, that his death had broken the lineage of association with the spirits, was no comfort, and any vanquished trepidation quickly resurfaced.

The three boys felt only the lingering contention between each of them and the devotion they had no vocabulary for, but which might have been love. They knew they intruded on these final family moments but followed from behind the group, fettered to the sight of Nena's body while brandishing heavy eyes to impress each other with their own sincerity. So that the family gave up trying to exclude them and Nena's mother, Maria, who had never succeeded in possessing her only child, stopped blaming the three boys for happiness life had denied her. On the threshold of Nena's departure she could sympathize even with them.

The family moved through the white terminal looking for the right check-in counter for Nena's cart of luggage, and Nena led them wordlessly, holding herself with more maturity or simply and innocently yielding to an unfolding concatenation. She remained herself to an exaggeration that made the eighteen members of her family wonder if she might not exist at all, but was the apparition of a common dream.

## II

Twenty-two years earlier when Balthazar left his mountain village under cover of night, he severed a tribal tradition that had survived the successive invasions of lowlanders, Spaniards, Americans and, most recently, Japanese. He was the oldest grandchild of the greatest faith healer of the region, who now waged his final duel with life on the floor of the healer's hut lined with animal skulls. Because powers skipped a generation at a time it was expected that Balthazar, and not his father, assume the life-language of healer and tribal leader. But an element of his thoughts suggested the age of healers might be fading. He made a last attempt at asking the unreceptive spirits, thought of confiding in his sister Maria, then instead without a word left to discover the world before it came to subjugate healers and tribesmen.

He skirted rice terraces hewn from the mountains over three thousand years, travelling south with the weight of his possessions tied in a bundle carried in his hand. Huts lined the ridges, stopping points for travellers or shelter for rice farmers, and in these he slept at night, huddled against chill and fog and the night tread of animals. Even on wet days he had few doubts. He was moving into the world, and in view of his new freedom it was progress. The terraces were familiar – gradations of green – but wreathed by fog they became staircases, and the journey, for all its discomforts, a climb towards something higher. He was crossing the abyss between thought and expression. When he rested, his mind cluttered with apparitions, the voice of his grandfather saying Listen for the spirit voices! So with light feet he kept moving. Occasionally he met another traveller or a hunter on the far periphery of his territory, but after only a few days of walking aspirants faded, vowels shortened and he had trouble understanding the dialects called out to him. This was now beyond his home valley where he recognized good and evil, and into the outside where he had heard that people embalmed enemies with salves that quickened the process of death in the living. Even if he didn't believe all the stories he knew people were hostile to the unknown, so he avoided villages and borrowed under cover of fog or night from their terraces the food he needed.

The longer he travelled the more he felt his journey becoming the path itself. If a carabao cart passed him, Balthazar asked the driver for a ride. Sometimes the driver, with skin darker than in Bal's village, took Bal with him a short distance, other times he was headed in the wrong direction, mountain-bound, or, perhaps deliberately, couldn't understand.

And in seven days Balthazar arrived in Bontoc, a town with a population of over a thousand and the first real place – the kind that could be found on a map – of his experience. A bubbling market, sandy yellow streets and grey houses solid as rock impressed on him things he had heard. His father had warned him of cars – metal carabao – now he saw a few, wheeled rectangles carrying a dozen people, trailing dust, honking animal cries at people on the street.

Others also wore tribal dress but Bal seemed the most conspicuous. Children gathered at his confusion, as if they could read the illiteracy in his face, know this was a man who could just as easily have stepped out of another time.

"Give me." One young girl with long, pitch-black hair held out her hand and smiled crookedly. She wore clothes made by machine, smudged, dirty, faded. Another girl wore nothing at all, and the two

lingered until it was clear Bal carried no hidden wealth of sweets or
money, that beyond what they saw he could offer no spectacle.

People walked to or from tasks, calling out loudly, carrying
produce or an enduring look of purpose that withered him. A short,
black-skinned man shouted at him things he couldn't understand. The
day was hot.

Fatigue had layered him, and now that he was somewhere rather
than on the way, he had forgotten why he'd come. Settling against a tree,
he exhaled and closed his eyes. Somewhere among those he loved he felt
a dawning absence. The ground shuddered beneath him as the dream
came too quickly, in a rush of mountains.

Wind circled him to block the dust, the noise of people and the sky.
Earth trickled away revealing solid light, though he still sat in shadow
and wind, his hands dark. Then a strangeness hit from behind, thrust
him onto a lush plateau amid mountains and sun, and his hands were
gold. Cries of birds drove him out of himself and he flew above and
underneath and to either side, watching himself dissolve until there was
only the plateau, which he could see but no longer feel beneath him. He
bit and clawed at this absence until he touched the foliage again, cursing
the birds for their intrusiveness. But he was returned, which for the
moment was enough, and he wandered off the plateau, through valleys
and back into this town that was even stranger.

Balthazar woke beneath the tree without remembering his dream
but aware his grandfather had passed away. He had died a few moments
earlier on the sanctified floor of the healer's hut lined with animal skulls
– his death flight had reached Balthazar's sleep.

Bontoc overflowed with its faces of market life. The heaviness of
death kept him from rising until the shade shifted, rolling skies traced
the leaves above him and finally a woman introduced herself to him in
his own language. *I've been watching you, and there's work if you need it,*

her mouth was saying, and he nodded, suspicious of her existence or her intentions. Her red and black tribal dress covered her ankles but not her broad arms. The face was round, almost a complete circle, creased into an ambiguous age.

"I travel," he said, to extricate himself. "Why would I need work?"

The woman took his hand. Despite her insubstantial appearance the fingers in his were solid and wiry. Her body exuded warmth. It felt the closest he had been to a woman since childhood. She led him through fields to a plantation bordered by hills and river. A few men laboured in the distance. Nearby stood a long beaten tin house. Mist dewed at his face. He turned to the woman to ask the questions condensing on the dawn of his thoughts, wondering if what they had been sharing was love, but she was already fading the way they had come. The hand she had released felt very empty. A bird cried above, in its flight tracing the path of a half-day's sun. The blueness resembled a sea he had only ever imagined.

A man too tall for the mountains emerged from the house, his loose clothes unwashed, not surprised to see Balthazar. "You are looking for work," he said in a tone that could have been a question or an answer, and rested his long face into a solidity that whispered a little out of kindness.

A current of indecision flowed over Balthazar's body. Its expansion of time slowed him into a serenity of dispassionate judgement. He had nowhere to go. Any past could be discarded, any future could be his if he followed its undulations, and this might be as good a start as any.

So he joined the small platoon of strangers who worked in that field picking cabbage, a vegetable few of them knew, and lived communally in the long shack. A few came from north and could be vaguely understood, others came from elsewhere in the mountains and might have been his enemies. He didn't recognize the names of their villages – Concepcion, Talisay, Bangaan – but origins here faded into a common circumstance. Workers kept mostly to themselves, picking cabbage until dark halted work, falling asleep, waking again with the light. Sometimes they shocked Bal by breaking into song, which in his village had been reserved for times of intense joy or intense grief, but here was used merely to break the dependence on habit for substance. Most returned to their home villages when they had earned enough for the return journey and to buy the radio, tool, medicine or seed for which they had come. To Bal, who had only rarely seen money, the wages the tall man paid him seemed generous, but others assured him they weren't. It seemed a reasonable arrangement, though: hard work brought him insight as he slept and would give him the means to follow what his dreams suggested. And around him in his sleep, amidst the snores and smell of the land, were feelings the same as his.

# III

With his small bundle he boarded a bus brimming with people and stood for the nine-hour journey to Baguio. Within four weeks of cabbages, abstaining from rum and cigarettes, he had earned enough for the fare. Along the journey an old man fell off the roof and they had to wait until he had clambered on again, embarrassed by the attention. The slow sway of the creaking bus over potted dusty paths lubricated tongues, and the hens scolded their caged chicks, men their restless children, women their drunk husbands.

In Baguio Bal emerged into a whirl of activity. People on streets sold motorbike repairs, rice, mangoes, offered young girls or moved with a sense of urgency even Bontoc hadn't exposed him to. He walked through the city looking for what it could offer him, or escaping what frightened him. Traffic sped over solid roads coughing dark clouds. Market rice was a shorter grain, vegetables went beyond valley greens or cabbage – colourful peppers and sprouts that never made it to the higher mountains. Even the sun was hotter, the air thicker. Men with missing limbs stood on the walkway gasping for pesos in incomprehensible tongues, stroking the worn strings of battered instruments, a cup on the pavement their only audience.

Balthazar bought a bowl of rice and dormitory spot with money left from the bus ride. A cot on the floor, previously slept on by hundreds of travellers and labourers, easily rocked him into sleep. In his dream the devils shadowed children around a bright garden, where one laughing boy, unaware, was about to be taken. There were two directions the boy could go, and when he moved on again there were two directions, the choices forking again, but in each case the boy chose wrongly, as his fate became tragic.

In the pale shreds of morning Bal washed his face to rinse himself of his dream. Stepping out into liquid sound, a street flooded with the activity of a multitude, he waded through options continuously being revealed to him.

Moving through the alleys, he looked into a barber's shop where a few schoolboys lined the wall waiting for their turn in the chairs. The mother of one was lecturing him, one hand moving from her hip to wave a finger in the air, and the young face with its shading of bored irritation reminded Bal of himself when he was a child not understanding a word his grandfather taught. The association made him sympathize.

Entering, he said to one of the barbers, "I'm looking for work." Work, he had realized, was the compromise one made with a city in order to stay. The barber jerked his head to a large flat-nosed man reading a newspaper in the back. Balthazar didn't know many words in Tagalog but had practised these with the cabbage-pickers in Bontoc.

Like all words they seemed a clumsy mask worn by his thoughts, one he couldn't remove because it had grown onto his face.

The man folded the newspaper, exhaled through flat gaping nostrils and handed over a pair of scissors fringed with rust. He called one of the schoolboys over, sat him in a chair, then returned to his paper and didn't look up again until Balthazar had finished.

Bal couldn't understand the schoolboy and had never cut a hair in his life, but he scissored straight, blended the greasy layers as well as he could, shaping around the ears and scraping fuzz from the back of the thin, brittle-looking brown neck. When the boss looked up after twenty minutes he said nothing at first but his hard eyes seemed satisfied.

Bal was awarded the job but felt little joy. Life being the ever accessory to death, he could only attribute his continuing good fortune to the passing of his grandfather. He settled into work, though, with a professionalism rare to local barbers, over time resisting demands and judgements through the daily stench of dirty hair, the dust of snipped follicles, clinging to his principles but without impressing himself.

In eighteen months in Baguio he rented a room by the botanical gardens and fell in love with a fruit vendor's daughter. They met hovering under a blood-red hibiscus in the gardens, but the affair might have been an erotic dream from which he awoke one morning in his own sap, dazed and conscious that he still sat on the Cordillera while the future waited for him by the sea. His attempt at a home hadn't pacified the ideals of the boy he'd arrived as or the ambition of the man he'd become. Seeing this restlessness in him, his lover filled in the depth of her love day by day, and her durians, rambutans and mangoes in turn lost their power to seduce. The memory of their garden hibiscus was no longer enough. Though he had known nothing of love or jealousy or passion before, he could understand her disappointment, the something hoped for not happening, and was sorry for her, and for himself that he hadn't been able to make a claim on her future. He wasn't solid enough, and she needed a man whose finished structure she could lean against to feel the comfort of a permanent shape.

Giving his landlady two hours' notice and without making a claim on his deposit, he left one day by midday bus bound for the capital. It was his second bus journey, and he hoped it would be followed by a second romance, or a third start at life. He was a different Bal from the one who had trekked through the terraces, over the hills, but still felt like an adolescent in an adult world, and for an instant he blamed the spirits who should have guided him in childhood. It was for them he had sacrificed any other, more practical education, which would have been helping him now as he stepped into the unknown.

Forces continued to lead him even after his arrival in the hot Manila night. The city was dark and immense, with no feeling of stillness, only a constant, subtly undulating flow. Following suggestions in his mind the unlit streets passed beneath his feet. He moved through the night looking in windows, listening for distant sounds. A small hotel appeared, walls peeling inside and out, whose old proprietor, also a man from the mountains, took one look at the entering traveller and offered him a free room.

"This won't happen often in Manila," he added as he handed Bal a small square towel, a half-used bar of soap, the key and directions through the house, "but the mountains look after their people."

*I've finally arrived*, Balthazar said to himself later, as he lay in his bed gazing at patterns of mildew playing themselves out on the ceiling. *From here I can go anywhere. Even America*. And at the threshold of sleep he was pleased with himself. He might be near the centre he had sought.

# IV

He spent three weeks trying to learn from a city that refused to teach. On the second morning he took a ride to the sea he had never seen, a silver horizon seamless, infinite, and digging his hand into it he had a sacrilegious thought. As the salty water poured through his fist like a tradition through its history, he wondered if rain and river were enough water to balance the world of the mountain man. The ocean was filled with presence, and perhaps in its currents lay the clues to understanding life and death.

In the National Museum he saw a travelling European postmodern art exhibition, relieved to read as much perplexity in the faces of other visitors as he felt in his own. Looking for the spirits his grandfather had known he visited cathedrals, temples, mosques – but their gods were too distant and abstract. How could anyone worship merely on faith? He saw an American movie in a shopping mall cinema with four hundred other people, shocked that the cruel bleeding murder and blown-up angles of naked white flesh shocked no one but himself. Twice in the street he saw women's handbags stolen – men galloping away with them as people looked on passively – and once in a jeepney saw a hand reach in from the pavement to pull a necklace off a young girl's neck. When much of his own money was stolen out of his shirt pocket somewhere between Intramuros and the Chinese Cemetery, and the hotel owner began charging him, Bal looked for work again in barber shops.

In the morning's *Abante*, though, Balthazar found mostly ads asking for cooks in rich people's homes. In his life he had only ever cooked simple things, soupy rice, boiled vegetables; the fruit vendor's daughter, before her passion had wearied, had taught him *adobo* chicken or *pancit*. But he saw no harm in trying. When he called the first number a voice with a foreign accent scheduled him for an interview and gave him directions to Quezon City, a wealthy residential district of the capital.

The following day a jeepney dropped him off at the biggest house he had ever seen, in front of a gate he couldn't open. A neighbour's gardener showed him the intercom, which seemed yet another incremental step in the mechanization of city people. Interviewed in an expansive kitchen with a white tile floor by a Swede named Nordströmer, a large man with an imposing smile who owned a crafts export company and a shrimp farm on Negros, Bal felt at ease as he rattled off references and talents he was unaware of himself.

"My master," he concluded, "following my year-long apprenticeship suggested I move to Manila where my talents could be better appreciated."

Nordströmer awarded Bal the position without asking for a cooking demonstration, perhaps to avoid admitting his Tagalog was worse than Bal's.

The family of the house consisted of the Swede and his wife, who wore a head scarf and came from Jolo, an island in the far south, and their three freckled mestizo children. They smiled at him more often than did the maid, Lourdes, who came three days a week and didn't smile often, but whose skin, in certain reflections, might have glowed at him with amatory intent.

Commuting every morning from a rented corrugated tin ghetto shack in Tondo by the bay, he began learning to be the cook he became, by instinct inventing meals from saltwater fish he had never heard of, using the right combination of spice, inspiration and convention to please the palates of the house.

And when he'd mastered the language the children clambered over each other after dinner to listen to his tales. His own life had become a story that could finally be told, but mostly he spoke of his grandfather, a man who had been able to conjure rain, sun or spirit, heal the ill or raise to life those who died prematurely. They, in turn, retold their father's stories of his homeland, where white giants walked discretely through wide open spaces and tall skies, where for an entire season the sun always shone or didn't shine at all, where everyone had a home and no one was hungry.

Bal became a fixture of the household. He saw his thoughts reflected in the mirrors hung in every hall. Over the objections of Lourdes, Nordströmers offered him a room in their house, and he moved to Quezon City thinking this might be as good as a mountain man's life could get. But for the first time since he left the village he suffered the worms of uncertainty and boredom. The world held so many complexities, and every possibility was presented with an overtone of vagueness. He was familiar here, yet an aberration, and worried the absence of conflict might find expression in an unkind dream. In his three years as cook he had impressed the family with his meals, the children with his stories, but now no longer remembered what had carried him this far. Perhaps the past could never entirely be left behind. Home for him had become the comforting concept of change, or self-discovery; this time he wondered if his relatives were well.

Nordströmer, horrified by the thought of his wife cooking during the interim, uneasily granted Balthazar's request for two weeks' leave to visit his family. "You deserve as much," he said, "but hurry back because we won't cope, and the children ..." He trailed off, his permission on the verge of dissolution.

# V

Improvements had been made to the roads and buses, but four days and three nights passed before he began to recognize the contours of vegetation and terraced slopes and knew he was here, walking again through the valley of his childhood. It seemed less oppressive now than then, his steps falling to rhythm with the sounds of the mountains. Only the green was less green, the rice from any distance lacked its fire, a haze hung over the clarity that should have been emerging.

He descended on a village close to dusk. A silhouette recognized him from afar, and out of a rushing purple form his mother solidified, pressing her face into his shoulder, arms around his waist. It was a tenderness he couldn't remember from all the enforced austerity of his childhood; affection could have spoiled a future healer. His father came and pulled them apart angrily. "Jhunior, how could you leave us?" His face curled into a snarl of shadows, but his severity also didn't withstand the occasion. He embraced his son beneath trails of cloud, and wouldn't let the air separate them. Relatives caught a glimpse of their traveller only after nightfall, when the reunion was reflected in a star, and the moon burned in the mind on lost memories.

The evening carried conversation, tears, even laughter, so long absent in the village but now made easier by the Tanduay Rhum brought from the capital. Bal and his younger sister Maria were the last people awake. Only the occasional stirring of invisible forms disturbed the stillness of the valley, but they were surrounded by silent ridges and could hear the drip of condensing mist.

A knowledge long withheld needed to be spoken. Maria looked through the depth of the hut for an outline of her brother, but shapes had lost their glistening, night had reduced people to voices and sighs rising and falling like birds against the evening terraces.

"Grandfather gave me a message before he died," she began. "Meant for you." The edge of the issue mapped, she headed deeper into remonstrance. "He died horribly, angering for life. His words screamed! He had made a mistake or the spirits would have kept you here. And in the weeks and months after his last life spirit passed, the crops shrivelled, no children would be conceived, the weather didn't follow the seasons and Auntie Nena and our young cousins died from illness. I had to walk to villages across the ridge pretending to be a healer so we'd have rice to eat. But I don't have the powers." She sat back. The sentiment behind her anger had softened her. "I misled."

"Then it's good I left," Bal said, still shaken. Venturing home, he had expected some anger lingering, some guilt surfacing in himself. He'd never thought he would return only to sadness and loss. "I would have been as helpless here as everyone else. Now I can help."

"It's all because you left! The powers left us then."

"The powers left us when Grandfather died."

"And they would have entered you. That's how it has always worked. The ancestors needed you to need us and instead there was an emptiness no spirit could fill. You left and our history died."

It wasn't that he had left – time had carried him away like the wind blowing a dead leaf. Throughout his childhood Grandfather had tried to show him the herbs, teach him chants, indoctrinate him to the *ways*, but his lessons had meant little. Grandfather had said whether he wanted them to or not the spirits would speak in his mind, but he'd been wrong. Bal had followed their suggestions when he'd needed a guide, they had whispered to him a trade in every town … but they'd never brought the forces of the world around like for Grandfather.

"I don't know," Bal said in his defence. He didn't have the powers either. He could never have been a healer, patching holes in time, maker of things yet to be made. This way he'd been able to become his own person. He could speak with his own speech. "What good are spirits if they come only in shadows and in dreams?" His voice solidified. "They never wanted *me*."

"You must choose the spirits before they can choose you." Maria threaded a barb into her voice. "Now we have no rice, the sun no longer shares our work and the spirits haven't been with us for five years."

In childhood Bal and his sister had held the same vocabulary of imagination. Their dreams had aimed for the same stars. Now despite all the loss the village had endured it pained him that she was the one still clinging to the belief he'd abandoned them.

"I'm here now," he whispered.

"You were selfish! Grandfather's message was this: you can't try to cross the waters or the ways of the healers will be lost. When you stop following a direction laid by time, the direction stops. The family can't separate from the chosen leader. We suffer, the earth suffers."

The exact words had been forgotten, but the meaning and urgency were as clear to Maria now as when she had made the final prayers and her grandfather the final command. She wondered if it was already too late, if the waters that couldn't be crossed referred to the body of spirits that had protected their village, if the fate of the family now was to drown in this horrible hard reality her brother had wrought.

"I can't stay," Bal hissed. It was done; if he'd left them to sink into a hell he must lead them out of the mountains. "My place is in the capital or beyond it. I have a job, there's a future I have yet to become. There's nothing *here*." He finished with a vague bitterness, raising hands he couldn't see in the dark.

"Then we'll have to go with you," Maria said.

# VI

By the time the Japanese had withdrawn their massacres from the highlands only two extended families inhabited the village. When the Del Rosario clan packed up to make the long journey to Manila it meant the end of an association that had continued as far back as memory reached. Although De Lacugos inherited the abandoned huts and fields, it was small consolation for the loss of their partner in the joys of many generations and in the miseries of the past five years. For Del Rosarios the departure was even more difficult; they left not in anticipation of a better life but because Bal, their designated but long-absent leader, assured them it was best, that when life improved in the Philippines it would improve in Manila first.

Balthazar's grandmother couldn't bear the transition and cried for the loss of her village, for the loss of her husband who had been able to heal pain, and for the loss of the soft pink cloud that floated beyond the ridge the morning of their departure. She died in the muggy lowlands three hundred kilometres north of Manila and was buried in the shadow of Mt Pinatubo.

Though Balthazar had moved into the Nordströmer house he had kept the corrugated shack in the Tondo ghetto in anticipation of such a need. But the twelve-square-metre assemblage of tin plates resurrected from the dump couldn't accommodate seventeen sullen family members. Nordströmers were kind enough to let a few women sleep in Balthazar's room in their house until a makeshift second level to the shack and bamboo annex could be completed in Tondo. Lourdes the maid grumbled at the extra work, the usual glow in her skin dimming into a grudging pallor.

Highlanders weren't made to feel welcome in the ghetto. When the youngest of the family wandered the alleys, whispers of *igorot* – of the mountains – cut unkindly through the air along with the smells of untreated sewage, fish drying in the sun and the layers of oil from Manila Bay. Members of the family found low-paying work as jeepney drivers or roasted peanut vendors, but most couldn't bear to leave the shack, imprisoned by glares, overwhelmed by the erosive currents of people outside the door, weakened by heavy, clotted air, by an altitude level with the sea.

After a year in Manila, one hardship more serious than poverty became apparent: the family was still sterile. Before Balthazar's departure over six years ago, almost once a year a new life had joined the family; now none would be conceived. Balthazar started to worry this might be the enduring retribution for his abandonment of the village; the others were long sure of it.

One night Bal went out alone, to sit under stars looking across the water. The usual floating litter, smell of death, were obscured by darkness, and under the shroud of night he made an appeal to the spirits. Was it the choices I made that have brought this suffering on the family? he asked. How can I lift the cycle of misfortune?

No answer spoke.

Although Bal, resident of Quezon City, was seen in Tondo less and less, Maria and her younger siblings adapted quickly to the vagaries of city life. Maria's mother, also named Maria, worried her daughter might be a bad influence on her nieces and nephews. On Saturday nights she went out in ever shortening dresses, taking a sister along and not returning before dawn. Even after a new job in a Japanese shoe factory, young Maria continued to frequent the same nightclubs after work, and one night fell in love with a US seaman. He asked her name and she asked him questions in a broken, nasal American she had picked up at work and in clubs. He said he knew of a hotel nearby; Maria said there was no need for that, she had a home.

The relatives, suspicious of uniforms since the last war, were unhappy with the affair Maria brought home to Tondo, but they couldn't fault the young African-American from Indiana who on his visits proffered embarrassed smiles and modest gifts of hundred-peso notes or exotic flowers or American snacks in bright plastic packages.

He affectionately became "Maria's Negrito" and for a few nights slept beside Maria on the floor of their shack.

In free time Maria showed him the markets and taught him how to get the best price. He made vague references to love and a common future. But within two weeks of having met, his hulking grey vessel continued cleaving oceans and he sailed with it, leaving in the hands of Del Rosarios an orchid and a promise to return, and in Maria an absence she would never be able to overcome.

Nine months later Nena was painlessly born. Maria's Negrito hadn't returned or written and no one could remember his rank, or the name of his ship, and his name meant nothing to the US officials they questioned. So the baby was given the name Nena Maria del Rosario. Gushing relatives didn't worry themselves with the disgrace of Nena's illegitimacy; her birth brought the family's first new life in ten years. The cause of raising her unified them in the absence of home, the tasks of feeding and washing her as gratifying as the sweeping meanings they vested in the noises she gurgled.

Nena's charcoal irises peered out on a world that doted on them, in observation so constant that in those eyes she became the world, and what she saw or heard seemed to come from herself. It was clear Nena loved all human beings equally, frustrating Maria's presumption that children depended on their mothers. In this case mother depended on child and its limitless, unconditional love for no one in particular. Maria kept her baby in the shack, denied it society other than family, and later refused to subject it to the traumas of a public education. But little Nena from within her Tondo world seemed to understand more than most. Speech came quickly, though the few words issuing from the girl didn't linger, having the solidity of dreams. The relatives knew she could speak intelligent things, but if they remembered anything she said it was only as a word or two, vague fragments of an obscure observation on the colour of time or the shape of a papaya.

Even so, Nena had all she needed, seeming to float through rooms, into affections, a chocolate-coloured girl come as beacon of love, by whom restless Del Rosarios navigated towards ephemeral happiness.

# VII

On the day after Nena's thirteenth birthday a small man arrived at the Tondo shack, his white skin and matted curly hair suggestive of the river spirits of their belief. He asked for Maria del Rosario and claimed to represent the US Navy.

Maria at the door, tilting her head back, felt satisfied her complaints at embassy and naval stations had finally rewarded her with a visit. But the man shifted focus to the mestiza on the floor. Nena, sitting on the dirt surrounded by gifts and the admiration of family, looked up and said, "Papa has sent for me."

The man nodded. He handed her a thin parcel and with another nod retreated into the alley that had delivered him.

In the gift Nena found a pressed orchid, legal paperwork, a one-way ticket to Indianapolis via San Francisco and a letter addressed to "My dearest child", in which her father apologized for his long absence. He regretted not being able to return to the Philippines, but there were reasons he would explain to her when she arrived.

That week as Nena made her preparations, three boys catching glimpses of her from the alley or the market, one after the other, fell in love with her. They followed her silently at a respectable distance as naturally as liquid finding its own level. Though they had never been seen before they became fixtures of the household, sleeping at night with the rats in the alley outside the front door, never distant, hardly saying a word. Theirs were the only faces not lit up in Nena's presence, marked instead by the frustration of having lost the entire self to another. Each boy seemed to accept the presence of the other two as unavoidable, and though occasionally they cast doleful challenging glimmers at each other, any hostility gave way to resignation.

Nena said nothing to ease the suffering of the three boys or the relatives, showing no expression other than that of a compliance with the only dream she knew: if there was love here, then it must exist everywhere.

Even at the airport she spent the final moments within herself while the family floundered in the wasteland of time between check-in and boarding. The struggle against loss became so wearying the relatives were willing to release Nena into the world so they could start blanketing themselves in mourning. Even stoic Uncle Bal, recently fallen in a heavy, one-sided love with Lourdes the maid, had trouble confining the imagination in his emotions. Since the tragedies of being unwanted by his grandfather's soul-voices, unloved by a Baguio fruit-vendor's daughter, this was as close to insufficiency as he'd ever felt. For Maria, losing her child was the final insult life could offer after being forgotten by the father of that child, the only other person she'd ever considered loving. And for the family this completed a cycle of defeat since Bal had abandoned his duties long ago.

With collective self-control they neared the security barrier where they would have to separate. A pause like breath held separated them.

A welling tear gathering momentum finally slipped down Nena's face and dropped from her cheek. Smooth sphericity warped in flight and shattered as the drop touched the floor. On impact it also broke the restraint of the family. As Nena stepped across the barrier single tears broke into streams and Del Rosarios erupted into a low wail that resounded through the terminal in arching waves of approach, crashing over bystanders with all the solidity of grief.

The boys clambered over each other for the best pose at the feet of their love, who in the arms of her mother gushed a torrent of tears. Security guards, intent on separating the escorts from the girl with the boarding pass, were struck helpless; looking on the family they were overcome with grief. Del Rosarios found little consolation in each other's arms, weeping for their forgotten ancestors, for the battle of the living against life's injustices, for their baby being swallowed by the world.

Spreading circles of the wail struck a Dutch businessman bound for Vancouver. Interpreting it as retribution for his infidelities he choked on a passing emptiness and cried for the loving wife in Leiden he didn't deserve.

A boxer from Mindanao felt the swish of tears submerge his shoes, and suddenly recognized the finality of flight, the shearing of lives accomplished in a few hours of jet travel, and he shuddered at the uncertainty looming beyond the transition and the brutality of his profession. Discarding his luggage he knelt down in the spreading puddles on the floor, understanding the pain of the Madre Dolorosa, to whom he now proffered his soul for the first time.

An overseas contract worker in search of a better life as maid in an oil-rich country realized she would never find it. Winding the loose threads of her life together into a ball, she gently rolled it into the abyss.

A yakuza with only nine fingers caught the final, terror-stricken image of the one man he had murdered in his life, twenty years earlier, and all the other evils he had witnessed were no longer accidental but intrinsic. He wept for the man's family, for humanity's failures and his own inadequacy.

A Frenchman cried for his lost childhood and the memory of a houseboat tour down the Canal du Midi with the father who had since died alone and sisters who had married and moved away to leave their brother to his lonely fate. He couldn't view his adult life in any other light but as a wasted one, as a chasm spread around him.

At the moment the toilets began to regurgitate water and the streaming faucets in the bathrooms couldn't be dammed, Balthazar del Rosario realized his grandfather's mistake. The powers hadn't skipped one generation but two; the spirits had found another. He felt the call of the mountains as it had roared through his dream in Bontoc, and knew that beyond this there was nothing left of time.

When bodies floated up the escalators with the tide from a flooded arrival hall the three boys caught glimmering visions of their own mortality. Their tears and unchecked urine swilled with the salty currents flowing through the hall. They had waded towards Nena; now they swam.

In a final blow, the water tanks erupted, rumbling in a white tide over security equipment, through computers, jamming electric doors. As the outpouring of sadness conducted electricity through water through flesh through water through flesh, the boys understood their destiny lay not in harbouring a collective unrequited love, but was to escort the last healer into the afterlife, where her great-grandfather was waiting.

# VIII

They waited in the airport and watched Nena's plane take off. Bal blinked to end the vision. Maria said, "She's gone," but Balthazar looked at her and knew she didn't really understand.

Other people in the airport were preoccupied with their own losses and didn't recognize theirs. The family wanted to leave and Bal said, "You go, I want to look at the sky with the planes." And he knew they were puzzled but they took home the boys to teach them how to sell roasted peanuts. Bal was alone. Like most skies, this one was a light wash of blue. But it was frightening. Birds and planes and clouds floated through it in a whirl, and it went forever.

He could have extended the age of healers; a Nena unspoiled might have extended it, but it would have ended. Now if his niece ever returned to Manila she would return as an Americanized teenager, not as a leader of her people.

The spirits paid him a final visit. One wiped away the tear on his cheek with her wisp of a finger and said, We are going to leave now. You will be alone, just like other people are alone. Don't be frightened. There are many departures but none are final, they just merge into experience.

The darkening sky became the deepest blue he had ever seen, tinged at its edge with crimson, and he sat there looking into it just a little longer, before turning and going home.

# THU ANH

Alice's grandmother once was raped in wartime. Before the American War, before independence, when the French were brutal in their suppression of the Viet Minh, a force to which Alice's grandfather was allied. The French came and ransacked the family home, found no one but a young woman, a toddler and an infant, and could have bayoneted the children, raped the woman and burned down the house as a warning to the insurgents. But the soldiers were young, not driven by colonialist ideology or brutal by nature. They spared the children, smashed a few things around the house and, after a thirty-minute struggle, stripped and tied up the woman. Their officer waiting outside, first one Frenchman and then another had a go at her. One, ill with dysentery, shell-shock and guilt, was unable, and the second fared only slightly better, lasting about a minute before expiring. Then they smashed up anything in the house that they'd missed, and continued on to the next home on their list of addresses extracted under torture.

Thu Anh confessed this to her granddaughter Alice when she was so handicapped by dementia the rest of the family had stopped bothering to listen to her. She cackled in a strange and unsettling glee how the French had been unable to manage a proper rape, much less subdue her country, but Alice suspected the reason her grandmother was telling her all this was that the scar this event had slashed into her psyche had after fifty years not come close to healing.

In recent years her grandmother had changed. She preferred the safety of her room – once Alice's. No longer very mobile, mind no longer sharp, she was afraid of being useless since the last attempt by the family to send her to Thousand Oaks Home.

Since her migration to the States she had played a large role in raising Alice and her younger brother Zachary, but a few years ago Zach had complained that she kept trying to undress him to play with his penis. Thu Anh denied it but for Binh and Ariel it fit in with her peculiar form of dementia, which had turned her into a scheming, selfish, unrecognizable woman.

For some reason Alice thinks of her deceased grandmother as she puts on her make-up in the evening before her date. She is mildly giddy, not at the prospect of dinner with Aaron so much as her independence to make decisions, revisions and romances after eighteen years of growing up under her father's fiercely protective conservatism. Her grandmother, before mental decay rendered her a sad imposter of the woman she'd been, was the voice of reason in the household. Ariel was a warm person but not as meticulous a mother as she was a corporate strategist, and so she left those decisions regarding her daughter's decency to her husband. Only old Thu Anh argued in her favour when Alice wanted to go to a dance or football game or party with her friends, while her father shouted such things weren't befitting a good girl. In Saigon, he would say, there were only good girls or whores.

Before the American War the family moved from the North to the central highlands, an area still largely unscarred by civil war, where they hoped to forge a new beginning by selling kitsch handicrafts to the honeymooners visiting Dalat.

Then the US involvement further wedged apart a country already divided. Platoons of southern and American soldiers prowled the countryside in search of the slightly less brutal VC. So this, a Viet

Minh family in the geographical South, did what many of the villagers did to keep themselves alive: sent one son to fight for the Viet Cong and another to join the South Vietnamese army. When one force or the other came to destroy the village, Thu Anh could produce the papers to keep their home intact and everyone in it alive.

Alice's father, Binh, stationed in Saigon, came through the war unscarred. And while many US soldiers found girlfriends of convenience they sometimes ended up marrying, Binh did something almost unheard of: he fell in love with and married an American woman. She was the young wife of an American diplomat killed by a VC grenade attack while sipping coffee in his office.

Binh sometimes wondered if that attack had been the final act of his brother Phan before the Americans found his Cu Chi tunnel network and bombed the area so emphatically not even the bacteria survived. Phan, like two-thirds of his comrades waging their war from underground, was buried alive while living in the tunnels.

Ariel, Alice's mother, had decided to fight through her grief by staying in Saigon, avenging her husband's death by aiding the war effort. She worked in gathering and collating information from VC suspects, overseeing interrogation methods that bordered on torture. Binh – who spoke the main northern and southern dialects as well as the Hmong language of the highlands and a very passable English picked up in Dalat's schools and Saigon's bars – was assigned to be her interpreter.

Their love resembled a flower appearing out of the blackened napalmed earth, an isolated mark of beauty improbably growing out of the brutality of war.

They married when Ariel became pregnant. And when the US public stopped believing in the war effort and forces withdrew, Binh was flown out of the country with his new wife. While many of his countrymen were forced to witness the continuation of war, or waste years in lawless refugee camps, or board boats and sail towards countries that didn't want them, Binh began in Connecticut a life so luxurious and foreign to him he never became comfortable with it. His wife continued with the State Department and he worked as a court and government translator until he set up his own small fish processing business.

For a name they decided on Alice. Ariel wanted the name to fit her family's tradition for girls of using "A" names stolen from literature (Annabelle, Annika, Amber). Binh suggested Alice. A girl who could shrug off the sheer madness of the war, he argued, and return from a nightmare wonderland with good nature and innocence still intact, this was a girl he wanted to raise and adore.

Alice remembers one time when she was young she entered the bathroom to see her father not sitting on the toilet but *squatting* on top of the bowl. It was the first time she realized her dark-skinned Daddy wasn't the same as her friends' fathers but came from a place she was unable to imagine.

Binh had fought for the vanquished South, yet when drunk proudly told anyone who would listen that his long thin backwater of a country had defeated the might of American military power. Once at a barbecue a big South Carolinian with a Purple Heart stepped up, towering over Binh, and said softly: "We came to help your side because you were losing. There wasn't a single major battle in the entire war that we lost. Not one! We signed a ceasefire in Paris the North didn't honour. I'm sick of people saying we lost the war!"

"You did lose!" said Binh, unintimidated. "Whether the South or North had won, we would have cast the Americans out just like the

French. We would have fought to the last man, woman and child. We're unconquerable!"

Alice enjoys the dinner for the same reason she enjoyed getting ready for it. It is part of a new freedom. She can come home when she pleases, won't have to answer Father's inquisition. She can listen to Aaron, who studies law, who plays tennis and has the combination of ruggedness and inexperience that appeals to her. And he's a good talker. If he's a little too self-absorbed to be her type, she can respect the fact he'll someday likely make something of himself. He tells her that she's beautiful. He is elaborately considerate, old-fashioned, holding doors open and pulling out chairs for her – a sort of chivalry she's happy ended under women's liberation, and yet she feels a slight bit flattered.

Binh spoke Vietnamese to her when she was young, but she always answered in English, the only language that seemed relevant to her. Their area of Connecticut, of course, had its own Vietnamese community, to which her family was loosely affiliated. Even her mother had studied Vietnamese in her years in Saigon and could get by. When Grandmother Thu Anh and Alice's cousin arrived in America, for the first time Alice recognized the importance of this whining tonal language her father still dreamed in. They understood no English, so she made an effort to learn some of her grandmother's northern dialect and her cousin's highland one, and for the first time to speak a proper Vietnamese sentence.

Binh on his father's death returned to Vietnam for the first time in twenty years, shocked at its growth, at all the young people who had no idea what their parents had suffered. He was now richer than anyone in his highland village, so he donated a flagpole to the local school and financed the wedding of the daughter of a cousin. He toured the flashy resort town of Nha Trang, his old haunts in Saigon, deliberately refrained, however, from looking up old acquaintances, because it was too much for him to process on one visit. For better or worse, decades of war had been waged in order to bring about this. Sentiment lodged in his throat and he wept in the street for no reason but history.

When he flew back to Connecticut his mother sat on one side of him on the plane and his brother's orphan daughter sat on the other.

Because Grandmother Thu was always on Alice's side in family disputes, when the only viable option seemed to be institutionalization Alice was there in Thu Anh's corner. "She has to stay at home with the things and people she knows," Alice argued. "We have to learn to compromise, to accommodate Grandma's illness, which isn't her fault and which she doesn't deserve to go to *prison* for."

"It isn't prison," her father snapped. "Thousand Oaks has people who understand her needs."

"Only her family can understand her needs," said Alice.

When Aaron brings her home it's raining. He asks if he can come in to wait out the storm. She plays some music and cooks fried vegetables and rice, and drinks from the bottle of Myers's Rum Aaron brought in with him. When the storm doesn't let up Aaron says he once had bronchitis and has a suspect chest, and can he stay over, he'll sleep at the edge of her bed and not touch her.

Not until he strips to his boxers does Alice worry a little, and when he moves on top of her an hour into her sleep she speaks an emphatic "No!"

Undeterred, sweat beading on his brow, eyes bulging, he pins her down and says, "You can't do this to me!" and when he pulls off her pyjama bottoms says words including vixen and cock-tease. She half struggles, half lies mesmerized by the degree of his lust – or whatever this need for release, conquest or power is that has grown so extreme he'll resort to force in order to satisfy it.

She remembers her small grandmother, how she fought off two French soldiers for half an hour, how her father's family and countrymen fought off the might of two colonial invaders, and finds the strength to scream, to struggle, to wrench one arm fee, grab Aaron's penis and twist it as hard as she can.

And later she has the strength to go to the police, to sit in a witness box and testify against Aaron, to be a subject of aspersions by a crack lawyer who gets his client acquitted of attempted rape. And then she finds the strength to go to counselling, to regain faith in humanity and, one day, her trust in men.

All because her senile grandmother breathed the power of her people into Alice's ear, one night when Alice was still young enough to listen.

⋇ ⋇ ⋇ ⋇ ⋇

# THE LOST MAN

## I

I was sick, and this was home. Roaches ran across the paperboard wall in a hotel where patrons of cheap whores booked rooms by the hour. The corner fan couldn't stop the sweat that dripped from me even at night. A single bulb illuminated the windowless room and a sagging mattress on a rusted spring frame was the only furniture. I'd vowed to spend as little time here as possible but no longer had the money to pass away the day in eateries and cafés. And besides, I needed to keep a low profile. Perpetrators of grand heists escaped to Barbados or Rio de Janeiro – this had entered the folklore as truth. To me that made no sense. Southeast Asia was farther away, money lasted longer, borders were porous, officials bribable, it was easier to hide, to become lost – if you were running why would you run anywhere else? I was a foreigner in a city of twenty thousand foreign peacekeepers, civilian police and election monitors – and yet the air of the fugitive surrounded me and threatened to make me memorable. I was ginger with red freckles on skin white as glue and spoke with a stutter and had a slight limp and there couldn't be too many of them around.

My first week in Phnom Penh I felt fearless – I'd made it this far. In a nightclub I was anonymous. People had their own worries. This was one thing I'd noticed in life – you could be a junkie, a thief, a killer, but until you bothered people out of their own mesh of insecurities, as long as they didn't have to look at you and didn't need anything from you, people didn't really care about other people.

And after a drink I realized I'd been chased from one edge of the grand continent to the other, only to find the saddest place on earth. Young prostitutes danced across the floor in slowly shifting rows innocent and beautiful and sad. Lights strobed a discordant melancholy, music booming hollow-loud to remind old soldiers of the thunder without rain that had been their civil war. Having fought off the French, survived America's secret campaign of bombing the countryside to shreds, the brutality of the Khmer Rouge, suffered the indignity of another Vietnamese invasion – now they had to contend with the blue helmets with their exotic drugs and their AIDS. The former soldiers didn't know the dance moves, their bodies still used to the pressure of AK-47s at their sides, against their chests. Instead they watched the peripheries where girls demonstrated fellatio on Heineken bottles for other soldiers who might have been their enemy. The dancers moved in stutters, the clogged atmosphere their speech. Outside, amputees held out hats for all these rich people to fill, but they didn't, and in the back seats as they were driven away for love the girls wept. UNTAC peacekeepers became hooligans, interlocking arms, swaying beers, wildly throwing punches.

Three young locals looked as out of place as I did. Two mates and the girlfriend of one of them. One in a white shirt seemed to have invited out the other two, wincing at each new round of drinks that must have cost him a week's salary. But his girl, in a red minidress, of ambiguous ethnicity, with sad eyes, wasn't impressed by the display of wealth because she was talking to the man's friend. So the one in the white shirt sat drinking away his happiness that these two were getting along. Even on the dance floor the girl apologized to him with her eyes and whirled and jittered, her ankles flashing white in the multicoloured lights, drawing all eyes in the room, but afterwards returned to his friend who also apologized with his eyes, sorry for a feeling he recognized but couldn't control.

The ending was clear to all three now and after two of them left I could only feel for the one remaining who sat hunched over his beer alone, sniper fire in his inner ear from the days when he was still killing and far happier.

I knew how he felt, abandoned by the living.

# II

Lyudmila, my future torment, used the hotel once in a while. Her mother had been a Russian whore and her father a local customer and she had olive Eurasian skin and striking deep eyes. There was coarseness to her gestures and language but also an air of exile I identified with.

Lyudmila, being exotic, bright, stunning, did well with her business. She could afford to be discriminating with customers; she chose businessmen who owned cars and paid for nice hotels, those she thought would treat her with a measure of courtesy. Or UNTAC peacekeepers who could continue to supply the addiction they were responsible for creating. Sometimes, though, she offered discounts to local artists she'd taken a fancy to. Or a dock worker dark and strong. These rarely had much to pay her with, and on those occasions she used my hotel, which was dirt cheap, had no pretences, asked no questions.

She noticed me stumbling in one evening and must have thought since I was a foreigner I'd be rich like the peacekeepers. But I was destitute, and barely myself. I heard the knock and didn't move. It could have been the police, acting on a tip, though a simple hand would have been able to punch through the thin wall. The knocking continued and a sweet voice murmured outside.

I'd been suffering some form of chest infection for a few weeks and recently it had thickened into a form more debilitating. When I stood up sweat trickled down my bare chest and head throbbed and I coughed and my nose felt ready to burst forth a dammed-up well of mucous.

Wavering, I opened the door a crack. There was no chain lock but with one foot wedged under the door I pretended there was. She didn't say hello. Lyudmila stood in a long red Chinese dress embroidered with gold thread. There was something wrong with her eyes – a shade too glossy, not a sharp sparkling but opaque blur coupled with neediness. From long experience I knew what that meant.

She smiled. "I give you suck?"

Speech abandoned me.

"Only ten dollar, special price."

"N-no, thanks."

"You America?" She nudged the door open wider, lifted and moved my foot, and stepped into the room. There being nothing in the cell to comment on, gingerly she sat on the edge of the bed. The side of her dress revealed the length of her leg, brown, long, slim.

"English."

I regretted this as soon as I'd uttered it. Tell no one the truth and tell no two people the same thing – this was my modus operandi for retaining anonymity.

"Actually, I'm S-scottish," I quickly added.

"You no sound Scottish!"

It hadn't occurred to me a Phnom Penh prostitute might be able to distinguish British accents. I rephrased.

"I studied in London."

"You name?"

"Ian."

"Yee-yang."

"Yeah." My name was a lie but it was a stupid lie, too close, linguistically, etymologically, to the truth.

"I am Lyudmila."

"Pretty."

"You want fuck? Thirty dollar all night. Suck, ten dollar one time."

I felt so weak that the way she spoke pained me.

"No money." I showed her empty hands.

"Hand, only five dollar!"

I didn't want a hand job but didn't want the girl to leave. The life of a fugitive is bitterly lonely – the truth is impossible to utter and everyone a potential informer. No crime, no amount of money, seemed worth this life of isolating distrust, everyone an enemy, no one a friend. I wanted to be able to sit next to a pretty girl and talk.

I nodded.

She kneeled in front of me as I sat on the bed and put both arms on my knees. With her fingertips she unzipped my shorts, waited, then unbuttoned them, played with the fabric. I was too ill to muster an erection, coughing as her fingers curled in under my boxers and pulled them down, lying limp and lifeless even under the pressure of her hand and, eventually, her soft lips. I would have been horribly ashamed had I had any dignity left.

"Sorry."

She shrugged and yawned and waited for money. I rummaged round the room but could only find a single dollar, as well as three or four thousand riel and change in tattered notes she handed back to me.

"I come back," she said. "You pay five dollar!"

I left the room. I gathered up my bag. I smoked a cigarette. I shaved for the first time in ten days. I looked at my shaggy red beard in the mirror. I woke to the sound of scurrying mice feet that always scratched through the walls in the early hours. I had vaguely fearful dreams of home. I went to bed feeling miserable …

The day was backwards. I remembered it only in five-minute framed segments that travelled back in time. Then I was three weeks ago, before I got sick, before I would meet and fall in love with Lyudmila, when I had been a mere exile holed up in a cockroach-infested room lit by a single bare bulb, before love rendered me a human being again.

And now, being a human being again, I was unhappy. Sick and love-sick in a sweltering claustrophobia, I felt like a human form of the vermin in the walls, creeping, scuttling, lingering in shadows. My brain felt so swollen I was amazed it fit in my skull. Air could barely pass from nose to lung.

I don't know what I had. Tuberculosis, a debilitating form of flu, pneumonia, bronchitis. Doctors were dangerous, expensive. I let it get worse until I couldn't leave the bed.

Lyudmila, looking thinner, more vacant, came again for her money. She took my key instead. She returned with chicken noodle soup from a street stall and spoon-fed it to me. This kindness overwhelmed me and I kissed her hands, which she wiped on her dress on her way out.

She came again. Days passed but I don't know what happened in them. Only one thought came to me I still remember: Lyudmila and I had never once said hello to each other. We knew each other too well for that.

# III

My first memory at Lyudmila's flat was of her beating me. She'd inherited a Slavic fatalism that after provocation and the right drug – or its absence – became Slavic fury. In some ways we were a good match. She pounded her fists into my stomach, into my face, and I was so shocked I woke back into myself, pained, sick and miserable. I flailed at her pretty hand, trying to catch it, but swiped at air as she caught me full force on the cheek.

"I love you," I uttered through tears of pain. A Buddha head smiled down at me from the top shelf of her bookcase.

"You fucker you don't know what love!" She gave me another kick as her eyes glazed with hatred. "Why you have no money?" she shouted, before venturing out to her work.

My illness had worsened. I'd withered away to a ghost of the yob I'd been. Once she'd known I was dying, Lyudmila had taken me out of the hotel. That was her story. After all, I still owed her five dollars. She said the hotel owner's son had carried me out. They'd tried to take me to a hospital; I'd thrown a fit of barely conscious fury so they brought me to her flat, where she spoon-fed me during the day and disappeared at night.

Recollection abandoned me over the next few days. Lyudmila harboured a grudge over what had passed between us in that time. How could I be guilty of something I couldn't remember?

She complained she was now unable to get rid of me. And every time she came home I screamed she was betraying me with her whoring.

But she was somehow mine. I recognized her as the girl I'd seen in the nightclub my first weekend in the city. A sad girl in the saddest place on earth, making a mockery of a man's love because she could.

One night I mustered the energy to leave the flat. I hadn't seen the streets of Phnom Penh in weeks and it was a different city, bubbling and crackling with activity beneath the surface. I peeled away the filters and it was all revealed to me, the suffering, the laughter, the getting by. Eyes shining on the cusp of memory and tears. Faces made numb in order to hide a wound. Human beings reduced by so much war to a cowering, fearful, though still proud and resolute people. It was a wound carried by an entire nation, but instead of providing a point for solidarity it distanced them from one another. The guilt of the survivor, of not having stood up for the weak loudly enough to get killed. For living when a fifth of the country died. No one's family was still intact. No one at their core wasn't vulnerable, and if you whispered the right words you could see them break, right in front of you, like glass.

When I returned to the flat, Lyudmila was flying on heroin. Not an injection; I could smell the lingering fumes on her naked skin. A blue-helmet punter must have smoked her up. She was too far gone to care about covering up but hers was a body too beautiful for her to treat so badly.

I undressed and lay down beside her nakedness and the anger gave me a strength I hadn't felt in weeks. She'd been strung out for so long that all she'd become, except at those moments when lucidity returned to her for brief spells, was either the presence or absence of heroin. It had once been opium or hash, now it was the smack the UN influx had popularized. Back in Birmingham I'd seen the decline often enough. At one time she must have been beautiful and brimming with future, now the drugs were knocking out her teeth and wrinkling her skin and sucking the imagination out of her skull and replacing it with a need for drug. She felt nothing during sex, could no longer feel love, prized nothing but the money she could exchange for another high. As we made love now, as her eyes glazed and saw nothing, it didn't seem a huge leap to throttle her. She might not even defend herself, already so removed was she from life. Then I saw it not as a possibility but as a duty, as the merciful thing to do. What the poor girl needed to save her from herself was a show of strength.

The thought might even have been arousing, might have made the sex more resonant, except the knowledge that it would have been a murder devoid of violence, too full of love and compassion, weakened the explosion of disgust I felt. This was lovemaking devoid of feeling or meaning. As I subsided and she still lay there willing the drug not to fade, the thought came again, more calculated this time. I could smother her and walk out fairly certain I'd get away with it – no one would bother to find the killer of a junkie whore, especially not the foreign police instructed to maintain the good image of UNTAC. And then I thought: Well all this thinking is all well and good, Owen, but where's the action? It's nice to think of the charity in murder but when are you finally going to make good on one of your ideals and *do* something?

I hadn't made up my mind but as I thrust into her again I moved my hands, finding soft spots and weak spots, with my thumbs pressing into her where her body dimpled or creased. When I found her throat a strange thing happened: her cries which had been so mechanical and vacant found a little life. In the back of her last coo was a note that trembled and held true when measured against substance. Encouraged, I pressed harder into her throat and the change in her was sudden – her body awoke. Her pelvis rose up to meet me, her scream held a tremor of terror and a quake of genuine lust until I cut it off at its source, now throttling, not wringing her pretty neck but digging into it until it broke. But it didn't break, the human body is flexible, resilient, and there was no malice in my grip, just captivation. She clutched at me so fiercely I let go of her throat and let myself go too. Still she came, her body trying to hold me tighter, our bodies clinging together in a mixture of fear and passion neither of us had experienced before.

After that night, after I had given her the only emotional purity she'd found outside of heroin, she came to love me a little. We both knew it was for the wrong reasons, but such emotions can't be moved by reason.

The next time we made love it was a slow-motion twisting struggle for dominance she eventually won. Love was, after all, her business, and I was just a West Midlands thug who had nowhere left to run.

# IV

I was no longer allowed to venture out into danger. Somehow I'd gone from house guest to house arrest.

"I'm getting better," I lied.

"You a lost man! No me, you die."

"If you don't kill me."

Lyudmila had come home with a collection of pills in different colours and sizes. Except for the bubble foil there was no packaging, no instructions.

"Take these four hour then four hour again four hour," she instructed, holding up a tablet of capsules.

"What are they?"

She shrugged. "Anti-something. I say chemist you a sick."

"And the others?"

"When one work I buy again."

Dutifully I swallowed dry an orange-white capsule, a white tablet and a red liquid gel cap. Half an hour later I was asleep. When I woke, she had me pop another pill, movement blurring.

The days swam through me, carrying me along. I was a baby,

waking only to eat and pout or giggle, as Lyudmila spoon-fed me rice mash in my small corner of the room and stroked the hair from my eyes and fed me another pill.

Weeks passed and it was clear even through the mind's haze my chest infection was getting worse. Nights and mornings I coughed up different colours of phlegm interspersed with blood. My only reaction to the drugs seemed to be more sleep – troubled, dark tumbling fevers full of jealousy and rage. She wanted to turn me in to the police. She was poisoning me. She wanted me to dream so she could bring customers home and fuck them in the next room.

Who was she? She wanted me to stay – in order to keep me like a dog? Was her role to be my assassin? My torturer? Set to bring me home to England in chains? My wife?

Wife. The word rolled off my lips like a smoke ring. Lover was exotic. Missus was bland. Wife was home. Lyudmila was home.

"You're my wife," I told her and she laughed. Piercing rolls of laughter.

"You think girl marry you?"

"Not any girl. You."

"Eat more medicine!"

And I took more. And I kissed her. It was what I had energy for, all I could manage before I slept again. Sounds of her going out. Sleep. Sounds of two pairs of feet coming home, trying to scream but being too sleepy. She's my wife, you don't touch her! … And sleep again – drifting into a new dream, a dream in which I was dying.


And then one morning I woke and was normal. I'd always been either hot or cold, kicking the covers off in a sweat or pulling them up to my eyes as I curled in a shiver. Suddenly, after spitting out the medicine for two days and not eating, I felt fine. Not fine, but I was myself. Horribly ill, I was myself. And being myself, I was full of anxiety. I could ask Lyudmila nothing of the past and nothing of the present, because if I did, she would answer. And if she answered, I might hate her for what she spoke, hold her weaknesses, vices and profession against her.

"I have to leave."

"Where you go?"

"I don't know. Home. Prison."

"You better you stay."

"Will you marry me?"

"You a crazy!"

"I can't do this any more."

"You sick man."

"You're not so healthy yourself!"

This puzzled her. She took it as the ravings of a troubled mind that needed her.

# V

We married to keep me in the country. I was becoming known, the ginger who lived among them. Phnom Penh police didn't much care who I was but once they realized I wasn't with UNTAC they came checking papers, passport, to see what bribes were in it for them. I had no money, wasn't well enough to flee, so there had only been one option. Lyudmila was now Wife, dagger-edge of a word. I had her name. We'd gone to offices and papers had been stamped, money exchanged, words spoken, and it was, as far as things in Cambodia could be, official. My new name was Ian Maximov, a name I couldn't register at my embassy.

"Will you stop working?"

"How we eat?"

"I have some money, but I can't access any of it! They'll arrest me as soon as I try."

"No I no stop."

I went out for a day. I wandered through Phnom Penh, along the river, looking for something I couldn't verbalize. In the quickly averted eyes of people, pavement commotion, bustling market life, I saw the city as a body trying to return to life after trauma. If a car backfired all the tricks to induce forgetting were forgotten – the past came in a rush that crashed over people with emotion pure and debilitating. It made me angry. Where had the world been when Cambodia was bombed because of a war it was neighbour to, then raped by a cabal of its own people? The country now was an orphan girl, still adolescent but once brutalized to within an inch of her life.

In England I'd never had much sympathy for people. Everyone had a shot at life, and a few, like me, chose to aim it at themselves. They didn't deserve pity. But in Cambodia they'd never had a chance.

Angled golden sunlight sluiced over the roof tiles of a temple. A female form walked against the exterior white wall, in evening gown. As she faced west our glances caught, and in her eyes were people without names, children, friends, the terrorized. She was conquered by them all, and it was her only victory.

When I returned and opened the door of the flat I saw a scene of two animals, one behind the other, mounting. I left again, vomited into the gutter and wandered along the Mekong. The sun was setting on my life; the sky at its edge was mauve and orange and pink, and the river collected this blend in its ripples and whorls, bleeding. It was three hours before I returned. The flat of my imagination still stank of smoke and sex. Lyudmila was alone, half a freckled breast showing through folds of her robe and eyes redder than my beard.

"You better you don't see," she said.

I felt for her country but it had never occurred to me to sympathize with my wife. I knew what it was like to be orphan, addict, victim, perpetrator, whore. My outlet growing up had been in occasional surges of violence – she had sex to feed her and drugs to numb her from the pain of life. The fleeting warm amnesia of smack.

"Better you don't look," said my wife.

The next day Lyudmila asked if I had parents.

"I have parents," I said. "But none to love."

"Any parent you lucky."

When I was born my mother gave me away. She could have been a whore like Lyudmila, a young girl knocked up by her cousin – I would never know. I journeyed from hospital to orphanage to foster home. A couple adopted me at seven. They were English; they were *nice*. They couldn't have children and believed in an Anglican God. They were distant but, as far as their conservatism allowed, loving. Slowly they recoiled from the monster they'd adopted. I raged at the dinner table, fought at school, failed classes, stopped attending. I tried beer at nine, pot at ten, ecstasy at thirteen, cocaine at fourteen and heroin at fifteen. A fragmented person, I felt in the drugs the potential to make me whole. My Hyde nature thrived and overran the Jekyll sobriety. Different drugs suit different people and different moods. Those who need a womb to climb into prefer heroin. Acid I quickly abandoned – too many nights rocking myself in windowless rooms duelling with shadows in my mind and praying for dawn to break. What I loved was the top-of-the-world confidence cocaine brought. I got hooked, stole, got caught, went to juvenile prison. My father saw this as opportunity to extricate himself from his foster title. His wife called him heartless. He called me the devil and her a fool. By the time

I was released, twenty-two months later, my father had remarried to a plump, humourless Essex flower shop clerk and my mother had fallen victim to a weak and broken heart. Again there was nowhere to go. Rage followed me wherever I went. I'd unleash it on the unsuspecting and the deserving. I swore to myself I'd never lose my freedom again. Prison was a worse sentence than death, even the juvenile dormitories with their promises of reform and redemption. But again I couldn't escape the old cycle – I stole and fought and snorted and smoked and smacked and stole again, without entirely losing myself to any force but rage.

Until one eighth of cocaine, bought in desperation, turned out to be ground fluorescent tubing. Tubing mixed with coke, so I was too numb to notice it was glass. I snorted all of it. It sliced open my sinus cavity, which never healed. When I sneezed, blood and brain oozed onto the handkerchief.

My new break with drugs was permanent, I told myself, but the anger remained. It did things to me, and through me it did things to other people, bad things to bad people. One morning I woke realizing what had been done. In a rage I'd throttled to death the man who'd sold me glass and called it coke. To some he sold pure coke, to some only an illusion, depending on how much he hated or knew you.

Through the window I escaped the pounding on the door. It might have been the authorities, but was probably the hand of retribution. Even hyenas had collectives.

A Merseyside freighter brought me to Normandy. Air France took me all the way to Bangkok, and a hired boat from Koh Kong brought me into Cambodia. Coming here had been easy. Returning would never be.

Lyudmila sat listening to the truth believing little of it. I'd told her too many stories in my illness for any of this to be true. But it was safer if she thought it a lie. I just needed to hear it, just once needed to tell my own tale in order to understand none of it.

# VI

Then it happened again.

In a doped-up raging stupor my former self returned. Years of flight – and I'd been found by my own nature.

The pills had been doing strange things. At night I saw shadows moving through tightly closed eyelids. The forces pursuing me were getting closer, they were just beyond the door, they were in the bed with me. Lyudmila was cashing in on me. Her customers were Interpol, Scotland Yard, Cambodian police, who fucked her as another knife-thrust in my side before arresting me and bleeding me into a new killing field. The pain turned to a rage for vengeance, then subsided again into emotional exhaustion. After sleep, in moments fuelled by coffee or another pill, the anger rose again in a red and black fire. And this time it wouldn't subside.

I hid on the balcony, peering through the glass, when I was supposed to be out. My wife brought a man home. He was tall and thickly carved, his torso when Lyudmila uncovered it was muscular, and I knew he'd come for me. He was a blue-helmet, but from what country? Foreigners all looked the same. I decided this one was a member of the Argentine civilian police contingent. Lyudmila, I thought, capable only of loving rich men, artists or Adonises, would certainly love this man.

It was the same rage I'd struggled with all my life – unmanageable but slightly calculated. It waited until he was unclothed and eager and she was naked and submissive and he on top of, then inside her. Mind now lucid, with a morbid fascination, I continued watching.

The act seemed barbaric, the perfect violation. I despised them for being too weak to fend off the vices of money and drugs and desire, for not thinking how I'd feel watching them. Lyudmila was making noises she used with me; it wasn't just business this time. And the man was thinking was this not a fine prelude to arresting a fugitive. I didn't know which of them I hated more.

The door opened under the hand of rage. The stucco Buddha head in the bookcase slipped into my hand then came down again and again like a judgement on the man's skull, until both were crushed and bloodied and broken. I stood in shock, appalled not so much by the life crushed as the sacrilege committed. What no faith could forgive.

Lyudmila crawled out from under the blood, muscle, bone and plaster mess and screamed, "You clean this now you fucker!"

I ran.

I dropped the body in the Mekong, fled south to Sihanoukville. At the port I found work on a ship cruising Southeast Asia looking for places to dump toxic waste from Taiwan. They asked no questions; the international crew were men from hard backgrounds, we gave each other space. At docks I worked hard. On the open sea I cleaned the holds and sunned myself on deck. In Rangoon, from a government official at the port – in exchange for some explosive contraband I stole from the cargo – I got a fake passport. In Sri Lanka while high on hash I got my first tattoo, a proverb written on my left breast, over my heart. It meant something in Tamil about going your own way but later I couldn't remember the exact proverb. We passed the nights playing cards in the cabin. The men drank cheap whisky; I'd stop after two drinks and go out to watch the rolling ocean by moonlight.

Months later on a Romanian freighter I disembarked in Hull.

I expected to be arrested on arrival but my crimes seemed to have been forgotten. Or the passport was real enough to pass. Or I wasn't worth hunting down any more – just one drug-fuelled thug who had probably done society a favour by killing another and then crawling somewhere to die.

I touched English soil and breathed English air. For a few weeks I wandered. I ate a lot of boiled meat, potatoes, raw or boiled vegetables, or, when I finessed some cash, pub grub and curries. Rolling green hills were dotted with brick houses. I didn't return to Birmingham, never ventured to London, avoided cities. People were courteous and reserved. When they greeted me I didn't know what to say to them. When they asked me about myself I lied. It seemed a country out of someone else's childhood, not my own.

I found a job in the East Anglia countryside at a dairy farm. It was low profile but also what I needed, clean air and hard labour to ease the tangled pressures on my mind. To keep me preoccupied enough to escape the rage. In a corner of England where no one would look for me, where people were simple and far between, where I might find a measure of peace.

# VII

I made no friends, caused no trouble. I did my job and after it was done I read books. Once in a while I went to the coast to walk on the beach and look beyond the waves. On Fridays I had a pint or two at the Goat and Compass but left before time, before I'd be called into drunken debates that might set me off.

After seven years a man came to the village, then to the farm, asking questions. He had the wrong name for me but the right photograph.

The news someone was looking for me reached me days before the seeker did.

I should have run again. Flown to Spain, Barbados. The life of the fugitive was tiring; I didn't think I had the lifeblood left to do it again. I changed my mind a hundred times before the man arrived; I was leaving to so many places that confusion kept me on the farm.

He wore a straw hat and had a hard, cold face and was tall and looked at me in recognition of the photograph he'd been studying for weeks.

"You're Owen Conway-Jones?" said the man. "Ian Maximov? Someone is looking for you."

"You, it seems."

"This person is a woman."

"A pretty woman?"

"She wants to see you again."

An entire period of Cambodian exile came rushing back to me.

"She's in London," the man added. "She came to find you."


Lyudmila had drugged a rich customer – she knew all about soporific drugs – and robbed him, flown to England and hired an investigator to find whom the international police had for seventeen years been unable to.

We didn't say Hello, This is me, Do you remember when we …

We didn't say any of that. To be confronted by another so similar – fragmented, without childhood – is to look at your reflection without the buffer of water or glass. And Lyudmila whole was an even more partial person than Owen Conway-Jones. Something had eaten away at her. The way she dug her fingernails into my arm, the way she blinked back memory when the music turned, the way she gazed through me and, when we looked up at the stars, beyond them.

"I have a woman here," I lied.

She looked at me. "You have wife."

"To be my wife you'd have to learn dairy farming."

She laughed. Not happily, but grimly. For the same reason we could see into each other, we were incompatible.

And then she told me why she'd come. She told me and then she held her eyes closed, trying to keep from seeing. I felt no pain, it was just another horror of many inflicted and received.

My son was dead.

Lyudmila had given birth to a boy with skin white as glue. She showed me a photograph. Brown hair, not red, but the freckles were mine. Parts Celtic, Anglo-Saxon, Slavic and Khmer. For twelve weeks she hadn't noticed she was pregnant, and then some sort of spite induced her to keep it. She was ready to be a mother, to be responsible for another life. It was what she needed. But in the end she couldn't keep from the drugs. She shot up throughout the latter half of the second trimester and the beginning of the third. Yevgeny, as she named him, was born with autism. Asperger's. Something not quite right, too many neurons in one part of the brain, elsewhere not enough. Yevgeny was obsessive, compulsive, uneasy, moods changed in a flash. He saw things others didn't and missed things in plain sight. As if he lived half in this universe and half in another. Maybe his condition was for the best, she thought at first; he couldn't recognize his mother for what she was, couldn't understand that his father had abandoned him. But he was too bright not to see the pain of things. Changes in routine, bright lights, sharp noise, sudden touch, upset him. He asked a few questions but never seemed to get the answer he wanted. He took in more than anyone could process. At six he jumped from the balcony. It was four storeys; the fall didn't kill him, not yet. It shattered both legs and cracked his skull. Brain aneurysm. His eyes accused her every day for five weeks until he died. Not with anger; with disappointment. She had let him down.

And so Lyudmila had nothing left. Not even a need for smack. She was too empty even for that.

She crossed the seas to tell me she'd killed our son. Because she could never escape the guilt unless I executed her for her crimes against innocence. Or unless I forgave her.

But I was in no position to judge anyone. "In this life," I said, "it's too easy to suffer."

"You don't know," she said.

"I know enough."

We held each other for what might have been the last time. It was important, I thought, that we had a chance to meet again, to discover for a day or two who we were in another country, another life. In a sphere where I wasn't a foreign fugitive and she wasn't a whore. Where we were just lost children who'd had a chance to be found and had lost that chance. All we could do now was touch each other without bitterness and finally say This is me, This is who I am, I once loved you more than I ever loved myself.

All we could do was say hello, for the first and only time, before we said goodbye.

❄ ❄ ❄ ❄ ❄

# THE MOON ON THE WATER

In the daytime the castle is reflected in the moat. Five tiers of roofs stretch from a stone foundation, which rises from the water, inverted into the sky. Sometimes I pause at the water's edge to study the carp, who gape their mouths and flex their gills whenever a shadow moves across the surface. They are just out of reach. I can see their empty dark eyes, characterless faces, which seem to say, Come get me, end my tedious, mindless existence of moving in circles and gawping at shadows!

There is one large, square-headed orange old carp who seems a little different. I don't see him every day, though I often come to the water's edge and peer into its gaping blank fish faces. He has eaten a lifetime's worth of rubbish and bugs and scraps, bullied his way over the years to the top of the moat hierarchy, and seems disillusioned with his accomplishments. Lord of the Moat. What a victory! Having found the pinnacle as unfulfilling as the base, he just doesn't care any more. Or maybe I am reading into the only fish here with character etched into his features. The marks of age are not the same as signs of wisdom.

I like to ponder such things, since I have a lot of time to myself. You could say I'm homeless. I have no one to come home to. That fact would have once embarrassed me, but I can't say I have a hard life. I have come to accept who I am, to take pride even in my ugliness, in the fact I sleep in the shadows by day and walk silently under the moon by night. The inner gardens of the castle grounds are closed to people at night, and I feel like the reincarnated lord of the castle, roaming as a ghost through the gardens of human history.

When I do venture out during the day I try to avoid the packs of tourists. The groundskeepers, realizing I belong here, have long since given up trying to throw me out, but the tourists seem unsettled. They are not unkind, but I sense I don't match their wistful nostalgic concepts of what castle grounds should contain. What bothers me are their expressions of pity. Perhaps this is my fault. In my youth, I admit I was a bit of a scrapper, and all these years later my face still shows the scars of that heritage. I walk with a barely discernible limp. My posture has suffered. I am not as quick as I was, and the females have long since lost interest.

So the tourists pause from their photo opportunities to leave a half-eaten tuna sandwich in a place where they know I can find it. A well intentioned gesture perhaps – and I'm not in a position to reject it – but certainly inappropriate.

On nights after those days I feel offended by the world, I always pause at the edge of the moat and catch the moon's reflected shimmer in my eyes, lapping it up like milk. Somewhere gliding heavily in the water is that old square-headed fish. I doubt carp can live as long as we do, but in a way he is my contemporary. We came out of the same time, and now are in a position to look back on our life and understand none of it.

Which brings me to the loss that haunts me. Nobu is the only person I spent any time with, whom I could call a friend. The first time he came to the castle, about three years ago, I could sense he was different from most people – simpler, odder. I wasn't afraid of him. When he called out to me I kept my distance, but as he slowly approached I held my ground. When he spoke again I knew he wasn't very intelligent. Not as intelligent as me, at any rate. His brain lacked the very element that might have made him threatening. I think it even lacked the scope for a concept like evil, otherwise so promiscuous in people.

So when his hand reached out to say hello I let him touch my head. I hadn't felt human contact of any sort for years, and a shudder ran through me, along my spine. An involuntary rattle caught in my throat. When I spoke to him it was as if he understood me. He treated me as an equal.

For the next three years he came every week. I took to waiting around at those times I knew he would come, and we'd spend hours sitting side by side on the benches that overlook the castle's reflection. In his simple language he told me about the cruelties life had subjected him to. Not that he harboured any grudges. I was the one shocked and angered by the schoolyard tauntings, the parents who seemed more embarrassed by than proud of him, the pranks by former colleagues. As a five-year-old he had had a seizure that had cast him into a coma, and when he came out of it seven weeks later he'd felt disappointed to still be in the world.

Like any good friends we've also had our problems. To express my gratitude to him once, I wanted to give him a gift, a token to show the strength of the connection between us as friends, something I hoped he could appreciate. Of course, I had nothing to offer, and my old body was beyond its prime for catching anything extravagant. I was, however, able to snare a field mouse, which was no small source of pride for me. But Nobu reacted to my offering in a way offensive and hurtful, kicking the mouse carcass into the moat where the stupid stolid carp would have no idea what to do with it.

I refused to meet him for a month. He came pleading, and though he couldn't see me he knew I was in the bushes somewhere and could hear him wailing his embarrassingly vocal apology – but I held firm, to show that he had transgressed the boundary of etiquette that is the thread upon which friendships hang.

Finally the depth of his repentance – or my own loneliness – won me over and I showed myself again. I was equal to his capitulation, admitting that our customs were probably different, that I had no reason to expect him to appreciate my gesture of thanks, yet even so – one final stab – such differences between friends were something he had no right to treat with disrespect.

Things again became as they were. I offered my coat for him to stroke, and in times of contentment even curled up in his lap. This was something I'd never thought I would be capable of with a human being, but our closeness allowed it.

Now I regret our arguments. I can't take back anything I once howled in the anger of the moment, because I haven't seen Nobu for months. Our last visit together was a good-natured one, there were no arguments or misunderstandings, and I think I can be confident it was nothing I did or said that cast him away. But Nobu has disappeared.

I am resourceful, independent, I can survive this loss. But I worry for Nobu. He wouldn't have stopped coming if he were free. I fear those who don't understand him – who will never understand him as I do – have seen fit to punish him for consorting with old cats in castle gardens, for seeking out different pleasures than those the human world endorses. I taught him the uselessness of false comforts like money or station, showed him the meaning of independence, and we learned from each other of the warmth that comes from contact with a fellow creature.

But uniqueness in the human world seems a shameful thing. Thinking about it now, I am sure those who think of themselves as his family took him away – away from the life he knew, away from me – in the misguided notion they were doing it for the sake of his happiness. If they did put him in a home, they did it for their own peace of mind, not that of gentle Nobu, who had more peace in him than anyone.

I spend my nights again gazing at the moon floating on the water. Sometimes I go roaming, wandering without direction or goal for days at a stretch, but I always return at that time of the week when Nobu and

I used to meet. He never comes. Slowly I resign myself to the fact he will never come.

I must satisfy my need for companionship with that square, orange-faced old carp who is too thick to understand the meaning of my visits to the edge of the moat. I am offering my friendship to him. Perhaps in his own way, gliding in slow endless circles, eventually he will understand. Perhaps he already does.

❈ ❈ ❈ ❈ ❈

# PERFECT PITCH

They met at the DJ booth of a nightclub, and like many sudden, life-changing accidents this one seemed to happen in slow motion. She wore a bright olive dress that was incongruous with the place. Electricity in his abdomen caused him to migrate across the room. Dry ice mist swirled with the lights and writhing bass, and she was requesting a song by a German industrial band.

That's my favourite, he said in her ear. Dark hair covered the sides of her face and thin neck. Shoulders slouched slightly, head bent down, as if the weight of insecurity had once settled on her in childhood and never lifted. When she straightened, it was with a new confidence. Her eyes as they looked at him were two windows into a different person, and before they closed he entered.

What's your name?

Isabelle.

She frowned at the reintroduction of language and took his hand – he'd seen her intention before she had. What struck him was how small her hand was, a child's grip hardly large enough to link with his. They exited through the back door. In the car park she redefined herself again, placing a finger between his collarbone and neck. Sliding two small fingers beneath his shirt as far as his heart – he could hear it pounding, blood coursing through his ears – she curled them and pulled at the fabric, pulling him into her car. His hands ran from her ankles along the smoothness of her legs, under her green dress as she unbuttoned his jeans.

When he returned to the club he saw his girlfriend Barbara. She had stopped dancing and was resting on a chair to the side. Her bosom heaved wearily. Her face, earlier so beautiful, had now been exposed for what it was – the public face of the hollowness that walked around calling itself Barbara.

You disappeared for a while.

Headache. Went for some noodles.

I would have joined you.

You looked like you were enjoying yourself.

Feeling better now?

Oh yes.

In a far corner he saw Isabelle with the man she had come here with, a thin man with a long canine face, and he already hated him.


Manu was a sports journalist, a reviewer for the football pages. He had once been a promising young goalkeeper, though a lack of height, faltering confidence and finally a lower back injury kept him from pursuing the only future he'd ever valued. In school most things had come easily – good marks in sciences, girls, talent at painting and sculpture, perfect pitch in music lessons – but these had meant little to him compared to the dream of keeping clean sheets while in goal for Juventus or Barça. Goalkeeping to him was a lost art, the greatest, if undervalued, role on the pitch, exemplified by its greatest ever practitioner, the Black Spider, Lev Yashin. Manu would have resorted to doping, steroids, a life of abstinence – any magic that could have helped his reflexes or raised his height and confidence or cured his back.

Instead, teachers of almost every subject had pressured him to pursue in his life what they had in theirs. You have real talent at physics, one would say. Or, You're the most promising young painter in my thirty years of teaching. Only one in ten thousand has perfect pitch – it would be a sin to waste your potential at the cello. If you keep practising your butterfly, you could one day become a champion swimmer.

Language and words were his only mediocrity, and in the end he pursued those, because they brought him slightly closer to the sport he'd never conquered as a player. Or perhaps it was to defy teachers whose pressure to follow what they'd ultimately failed at served only to illuminate inadequacy as an overriding, general concept.

He wrote reviews of league games and a weekly opinion piece that was syndicated around the country. Perhaps his inside knowledge and intuitive understanding of the game had become such that he could have ventured into coaching or management, and for a while he was tempted. But he was waiting for something.

One summer while a second-string keeper in the national youth squad, he had practised for a tournament in Barcelona. After a day's training he walked to the middle of the pitch in the empty cauldron of the Camp Nou with eyes closed and arms out to the sides. Head tilted back, the 100,000 empty seats of the stadium began spinning around him, blurring the world until it was infinitesimal and beautiful. It was perfect – a feeling that rooted him to the pitch, to the history of the sport and human endeavour, until it was in him, a force eternal, strong enough to conquer death.

That was the feeling he was waiting for. To be able to recreate for an instant such a moment with his pen or his mind, to create a word or a paragraph with the ability to transcend this shell of his being and any feat in the history of recorded time.

He sat in the office trying to write the reviews for that afternoon's games. His brow was damp, and he wiped it with a hand likewise clammy. Thoughts conflicted and it was a struggle to break down in an interesting way three matches that among them had offered a mere two goals – sloppy affairs resulting from woeful defending. Even the companion pieces on the disgraceful rise in simulating fouls and injuries, or on the gratingly negative 4-2-3-1 formation, wouldn't write themselves.

He shivered, trying to avoid doing the inevitable. He typed another sentence, and it was a poor one, a standard pundit's cliché.

Now was too soon. She needed time, he told himself, to realize she needed him. His screensaver came on again. It was his photo, a blur of light in the dark.


He had been walking home after a party when his small digital camera gave an electronic click under a streetlight. At that same instant he felt a chill. When it passed he looked down at the camera, dangling from his wrist. He hadn't pressed any buttons, it hadn't brushed against him with the force to discharge it. Why had he felt, for the space of an instant, like a stranger in the world?

He brought up the last photo taken, but on the small screen couldn't discern anything at all. A blurred light in the dark.

Once home, he plugged the camera into his computer. Enlarged, zoomed into, the photo looked merely like a bigger version of the blip on his camera screen. He had almost expected some beseeching, ghostly cry from another plane of existence – even a curse. But there was nothing. Why had he been so worried?

The next day, using an edit program at work, he tried adding brightness, colour, expanding contrasts, and the streak of light became richer, full of nebulous fire like a comet tail. The background darkness grew grainy, speckled with particles of red and yellow. It was pretty, abstract, as interesting a photo as all the party snapshots from the evening. He deleted an unattractive angle of a drunken Barbara, a group shot too blurred to be interesting, Aurelio passed out on the sofa – but he kept that photo of nothing taken by a ghost.

Now he looked at it again. On his computer screen it could have been cosmic, like a space telescope picture of a distant galaxy. No, it was bigger in scope, even, than that. It was, he decided, nothing less than the universe itself.

And gazing at it he could think of nothing but the girl in the green dress.


He moved his mouse and the picture vanished.

He called her. She'd relinquished her phone number reluctantly, without wanting his, as if ever speaking again would have ruined the magic of their brief, mostly silent meeting. It was written on a tissue he held delicately between his fingertips.

Isabelle?

Yes.

It's me, Manu. We met on Saturday.

Oh, was that your name.

I was wondering …

I'm glad you called.

You are?

And she spoke a few words that formed a ring around the beginning of a plan, one he had vaguely suspected when he'd looked into her beside the DJ booth.

Now the eyes, the neck, the open eyes, the point where her legs had opened under the green dress, sad eyes – swam around his memory along with the scent of her. They would meet tomorrow.


As a child, she had known at eight what she wanted to become. Through great beauty or even great cruelty Isabelle wanted to be remembered by those who laid eyes on her as long as she lived and beyond. She knew this kind of permanence couldn't be achieved alone. In the years beginning with high school she'd been to exhibition openings, poetry readings, music recitals, looking for one who could be inspired by her to make a composition. Like a sitting for a portrait, modelling for a photo shoot or being a muse for a poet. But more than that – becoming the instrument a musician could play and achieve greatness with. Except the glory would go to the instrument.

Most of the artists she met bored her; the talent was meagre, or the talent was sufficient but produced only what was fashionable, what would please and evoke flattery. Either the imagination or the purity of purpose was tainted. One or two of them might even have been able to make a composition of the universe, but when it was finished it would have lacked the artist's own self. He – and it had to be a man, or a woman who loved women, inspired through her – would have remained outside, trying to project himself into a work lacking its most crucial element.

She needed not a sequence of projections but the truth. So she attended the events more to prepare herself, to attune herself to recognize the right one when he appeared. For someday, she knew, he'd find her. It was what she'd willed with her being as long as she could remember, like a softly struck tuning fork reverberating into history. Fulfilment would come at a high price, just like anything worth having, but she felt prepared.

That she might have found him by accident became clear only in retrospect. But then, nothing had ever been as natural as that night. He'd understood her, and with him she'd felt the change beginning in her, another creature waiting to become her.

At the cafe they sat and nursed their coffees. Manu spoke of the weather, of football and the Russian keeper Yashin, of food, but Isabelle's answers came in short sentences followed by long pauses. He tried a joke and she smiled. There was more meaning in the silences than they could digest. He noticed her fingers as she ate a slice of Black Forest cake. The fork dug into cake incisively, exquisitely, cruelly. She could have been dipping into his heart. When he couldn't stand it any longer he leaned over and took her hands in his. The fork clattered against the plate.

I couldn't stop thinking about you.

That's nice.

I'm happy I found you.

I guess I wanted to be found.

It felt like ... fate.

Fate is made, not drifted into.

Maybe.

There's something I want to show you.

She disengaged her hands and drew from her bag a faded print of a painting he assumed was Chinese. He studied it for a moment, unsure of its significance but impressed by its attention to detail. It showed a woman, lower legs bare, dressed in a regal gown atop a dragon, and before and below her men marched to consolidate the corners of the painting, representing all the provinces of the kingdom. He could have studied it for hours, the fine manes of the horses, bejewelled swords, wisps of steam from the dragon's snout, the dark, textured forest in the background, and especially the woman herself, whose features were delicate while secreting great strength. Even in this two-dimensional form, mounted and on the attack, she was extremely beautiful.

Do you know what this is?

Should I?

This was a great painting by Zhang Zhen.

It's still great.

This is nothing but a print. A print of a copy of a copy … a series of copies.

And the original?

Destroyed. It was Zhang's lifeblood, part of a composition deemed too beautiful. No one could look on it and not be conquered by its subject.

As if he'd sold his soul for art?

That's a Western simplification. The reality is more connected to the forces that tie all life into the same existence. Zhang used his spiritual training to tap into that. Wu later decided he couldn't be allowed to repeat his masterpiece for someone else, so Zhang was forced to kill himself. He knew the painting would one day be burned, its ashes scattered, but his lasting curse was to whisper its secret to an apprentice, who then could repaint it from memory. When the apprentice suffered the same fate, the secret passed to Li Bai, who painted it again in secret. Its power turned Li Bai into one of the most famous poets in history.

Li repainted every detail of the original painting?

The details weren't as important as the spirit of the painting, the inherent message of it.

What message?

You'll understand in time.

So Zhang could live on through his masterpiece?

Not him, but his subject.

This woman …

Wu Zetian.

Who is she?

The greatest beauty of her era, cruel in her ambitions, but she united and consolidated an empire.

The power behind the throne?

She didn't need to hide. She was the throne – she ruled for half a century, China's only empress. Over four hundred emperors, one empress.

And Isabelle told him the story of Wu Zetian, born during a solar eclipse in 625. As a child she claimed to have seen and felt a dragon pass by. As she grew up she had an all-encompassing talent. Her beauty and intelligence were noted by the authorities, and at thirteen she was brought to the palace at Luoyang, to be one of 121 concubines for emperor Taizong. As her mother tearfully said goodbye, Wu said to her, How do you know it's not my fate? She knew there was no better place than in the heart of the kingdom for her to achieve her ambitions.

The emperor became fond of her – how could he not? – but her determination worried him. She asked to tame his favourite horse, too wild to mount. All she needed, she said, was a whip, a hammer and a dagger. If the first failed to tame it, she'd smash its head. If that failed, she'd slit its throat. Taizong commissioned Zhang, the kingdom's best painter, to tame and feminize the girl by framing her beauty. Zhang came down from Wudang Mountain, and some said he was a wizard, though in truth he had simply tapped into the same supernatural force Wu had glimpsed as a child. Some of this force went into Zhang's painting, and instead of making her submissive, it made Wu greater than she was. In potential this power was infinite, but the painting was imperfect; in practice the power had to be harnessed. So Wu got down to work.

When the emperor died, helped by her poison, she moved on to his son, the new Emperor Gaozong. Before indifferent to her charms, now with the painting's power she was irresistible. But the new emperor had a wife, Wang, and a favourite concubine, Xiao. Wang was jealous of Xiao, and to gain favour with the empress and a night's access to the emperor, Wu helped Wang remove Xiao from the picture. But she didn't stop there. She went on to seduce the emperor. When she later gave birth to the emperor's daughter, she saw her great chance in the beautiful baby; she smothered it in the night and blamed the empress. Of course, it made sense – no mother would kill her own daughter; Wang's jealousy of Xiao, and then Wu, had been obvious; and a royal child would have elevated Wu to a level nearly equal to the childless empress.

Wang went to prison for infanticide. Wu took her place, and had more children to consolidate her position, and had those who opposed her, even the emperor's uncle, executed. When the emperor later thought Wang and Xiao should be rehabilitated, Wu in a rage had their feet and hands cut off and the women locked into oversized wine jars, where it took them a few days to die. And she issued an edict that to speak of the deceased was forbidden; no one could even utter the name of her former rivals – their existence wiped from the world. When the emperor died, again helped by her poison, she took his place, first using her weakest son as a front, then seducing those who might have sought to take her power away or crown a new emperor. Anyone who accused her of witchcraft was summarily tortured to death. When one of her sons later became too ambitious, she had him killed too, and herself crowned queen.

And so she ruled the kingdom, riding into battle herself to subdue unruly provinces. To document her extraordinary power and beauty – for in her it was the same force – she commissioned Zhang to complete the composition he'd begun so many years earlier. He was older now, skills more refined, and this time he set the painting to music, accompanied by poetry – and it became so overpowering no man or woman could look on it and not submit to Wu's will.

And Zhang was forced to fall on his sword – otherwise he might have made a rival tapestry. Wu ruled without opposition; it was the most stable and fruitful era of all of Chinese civilization, and she the most powerful woman in human history.

When enough men had fallen to its power, and enough time had passed, one brave woman found the painting and burned it, and had its ashes scattered. And so Wu lost enough force, past 80, to finally have to abdicate and die. But her spirit lived on in the burned masterpiece. For now that spirit was resting, but it could be reincarnated in another form.

As Isabelle finished the story, she looked at Manu. In her eyes a simple query.

Do you think you can do the same?

Consolidate an empire?

Create a composition like this.

Why do you think I could do something like that?

You're a writer, she explained. An artist.

I'm a football journalist.

You're the one who can paint me – uncontaminated and whole.

What happens if I do?

Then you'll see me for who I am.

What she wanted from him he thought he understood. He'd heard a similar story from his grandfather. In a way, Isabelle wanted his soul. Or rather, she wanted him to write down and glorify her soul. It was the same.

In my family, he said with resistance, from the gypsies there comes a different story, but with a familiar essence. And in its message a warning.

There's no warning in this. Only possibility.

Or impossibility.

It's your chance to become greater than you are.

Do I need to be more than myself?

Some people, no. You, yes. And – she leaned over, taking the hands that had earlier taken hold of hers – you'll know my gratitude and … understand my love.


To concentrate on the new composition he quit his job. The art of football was replaced in his efforts by art itself. Whether it was the right or wrong thing to do he didn't know. But Isabelle had been right; he had no choice but to try. Leaning over his ear, she told him in a whisper that beauty is something that exists in the mind, never universal, never observable second-hand or from a distance or from too close. The right conditions might only appear for a fraction of a second, but that instant will change you and stay with you. By causing the change it will become part of you.

He understood. Beauty was merciless. You didn't look at it; it looked at you and didn't forgive. It entered and took hold.

His grandfather's gypsy legend formed the kernel for the composition which was to become the girl. The print of the Chinese empress burned in his mind; he had no need to see it to recreate its features. He began with simple depictions of beauty. Part prose and poetry, part watercolour and sculpture, part music. This elaboration on art could have come from any era, with Isabelle as the fulcrum around which the universe rotated. These forces were to empower the model enough to make her more than human, to reach across boundaries of time and space. The beat of the music would mirror the beating of the heart, and when the heart sped up at the beauty of the melody, the melody had to keep pace until the perfect crescendo, beyond which nothing could exist independently.

When Manu was young his gypsy grandfather had first told him the old legend, passed down through the family. He told it in a tone of warning, and approaching his deathbed twenty years later reminded Manu of it. What the story was a warning against, Manu had never been quite sure.

Beauty once entered a village in the night, the tale said, to show people the face of truth. With her celestial aids – full moon and stars at their fiercest – beauty saw into the core of people. When women slept with their faces exposed, they burned with fever. From her corrupted stream men drank madness and death.

This beauty rose beyond face or body and inspired love beyond the love of romance. It involved the love of the father for his daughter, the need to keep innocence from harm; coupled with the devotion of the son for the mother, the need to prove your worth, to become. Beauty had no weakness and could command an army; no one dared disobey out of fear of losing their only chance to be loved. Once you saw her you associated her face with past pleasures, hinted or real, and dreams meshed with memory, so that when she chose to summon you, you couldn't refuse.

This legend came not out of the family or gypsy tradition but out of the memory of man – beginning with the first ape who gazed up at the stars and considered them beautiful, continuing with every creature who ever looked on something of wonder and willed it never to change. But throughout history beauty always changed. The perfect sunset faded to night. The most loved woman grew old and died. Even a breathtaking view died. Because the one who had appreciated it changed or died, or became hardened to the perfect vista. Or the mountain crumbled, worn to dust.

Now Manu had a chance to seek the right words, find the right touch to harden beauty into permanence, so that on recognizing it no man could be unmoved; it would burn within, immutable.

When Barbara appeared at the door whispering of unanswered phone calls he was angry at having to listen to anything unrelated to the perfection of beauty. The fact that he'd once loved her disgusted him.

You're not wanted.

What have you become, Manuel?

A creator. With no time for distractions.

And he closed the door on her tears, turning his back on the veneer people thought of as the world, that evil which had kept him divided from himself for so long. He was now delving into something deeper.

He returned to the room where Isabelle – *Isis the beautiful* – lay naked. She didn't ask who had been at the door; she didn't care. People no longer interested her except in their capacity to irritate, hinder or glorify her.

She turned on the couch with a moan, one foot sliding up its backrest and over, the other lightly lowering to the floor. Arms likewise spread out. Despite the posture she looked the opposite of vulnerable, and this visible strength licked a fierce arousal into him.

The twisting presence of Wu Zetian's dragon could only be felt as it swam through the room. It was an ancient creature, itself the incarnation of a princess who had once fought with men and slaughtered thousands. Manu's pen had written it out of history, and now it ate its way into the womb of the girl and gave her fire.

There were other pauses, irritations like having to eat, go out to buy more food, to withdraw money from a dwindling savings account. Living in constant arousal – the scent of her, bitter and acidic and sweet, like crushed ants and honey, was enough – they made love four times a day. Drops of secretions weaved through the house in silk-and-burgundy chains. He considered it research, delving into her depths, and every undulation beginning in her clenched toes, spreading across the geography of her body, brought forth a new realization so pure it might have torn through the unprepared like a thousand knives. In time he learned how to transfer this to his masterpiece, but it was a hot burning beauty that scorched the core of him.

He painted a scroll depicting a long-forgotten epic battle between the forces of nature and spiritual man, tamed a piano to cry in chorus at the beauty of suffering, wrote songs of love and the sharpest prose that could be fashioned. It was painstaking. Not one note or brushstroke could be superfluous or imperfect, not one letter irrelevant to the spelling out of destiny. He was weaving a panoramic tapestry of time, and when complete it would thread into and around him and conquer any man in its presence and beyond.

So pure became his focus that after weeks the original direction was no longer decipherable to him. The composition was still lacking a crucial, unifying element, but now its scope and meaning extended beyond its creator. He'd been woven into his own work, unable to see it from afar.

To discover what was missing he needed sacrifice, Isabelle told him gently. He was a shell of a creature caught in a shell of a world while the answers lay in the universe. Only by stepping out beyond the illusion could he gather the truth. For this he needed not the cure everyone sought but the wound.

Pain had to be rediscovered. To focus him Isabelle ran a razor blade along the dotted line of his spine, pulling skin apart to reveal bone and nerve and muscle and sinew and blood – warm blood that dripped into corners of the house or was captured in cups and with a brush added as pointillist shading to the rain in the composition. He noted the scent of burning hair and flesh as she guided a candle flame across his chest. What was the use of an ear, if the pain of its removal could crystallize thought? His body, piece by piece, was beginning to transcend itself, and each new revelation of sensation was solid, ready to be incorporated into a creation that was no longer his.

He ventured out, clutching a kitchen knife, to perform a sacrifice in the name of completing his understanding of the human condition. They had decided it would be a random act, an undertaking in the night, and on his return at dawn she would appear before him and reward him as they feasted on the new revelations and licked the blood off the edge of the knife. Then she decided that in order to bring closure to a history in which they'd been lesser people, the victim had to be either Barbara or the canine one from Isabelle's past.

But when he arrived at the man's house he found the door unlocked. He felt the same chill that had touched him after the party the day after meeting Isabelle – the wind of a passing dragon. Slipping soundlessly through the rooms, he discovered a heavy shape swaying from the ceiling in the kitchen. The dog had already hanged himself. Isabelle's transformation had been subtle, written out by Manu – now Amun – and even without seeing it this former lover had been able to feel its power and guess at its conclusion. He moved instead towards another's home, and felt nothing when he saw himself in her eyes.

Your first victims, he told Isabelle later.

No. They were victims of their own insufficiency. You'll be my first true victim. The first to lose yourself to me in all your strength.

The day he finished the composition she towered high as she took in the scale of it. She took his breath away. Long had he dreamed of preserving a one-goal lead; now he was exposing life itself. Their trinity of man, woman and art discovered they were one and the same, achieving what only legend could imagine.

This is how beautiful you are.

With one final gesture – one final expression.

Beauty slid her way on top of him so they fit together like parts of the machinations of the universe. She carved herself into him with the same kitchen knife he'd used to transcend a lesser woman. And she leaned over his ear, because he needed to understand one final truth.

I never loved you.

Isabelle's composition was complete. As life drained away with the blood seeping across the floor, staining the hands he raised to his eyes, he knew that if he lived a thousand years nothing would compare with this instant.

He'd uncovered the truth of beauty, and it was enough.

�֎ ✖ ✖ ✖ ✖

# ABOUT THE AUTHOR:

EZRA KYRILL ERKER was born in Berlin and grew up along the Black Forest and in Switzerland, of German, Dutch and Filipino roots, among others. Educated in California, he has spent most of his life in the Asia-Pacific region, with the longest stay in central Japan. Currently he works as a journalist in Bangkok. *Embers*, a novel of Japan, is also forthcoming with Orchid Press.